BLACK VIRUS

OUTBREAK

*FOR VICKY AND LUCAS. I WOULD NEVER
HAVE FINISHED THIS WITHOUT EITHER OF
YOU.*

BLACK VIRUS OUTBREAK

BLACK VIRUS OUTBREAK

Prologue

June 3rd, 2027 – New Candor Facility
Genotech, 13:00

Perrin hid his face from view of the cameras as he stood in the elevator on his way down to Lab 3. The harsh, white lighting highlighted the pallidity of his skin, and would make him easily recognizable, if he wasn't careful. Having only recently received clearance to be heading down to this level at all, he was considerably nervous to be using a false name. Add into that the fact that he was about to steal confidential, highly valuable material, one could understand why he was doubly nervous. He wiped the sweat off his brow, pushing back his auburn hair, but being sure to keep his face from view. The seconds ticked by as the elevator slowly made its way down. Two or three times Perrin almost talked himself out of it, but he stayed strong, the thought of the huge payout he would receive was more than enough motivation.

Maybe Genotech will learn to treat their interns better after they lose something this important, he thought bitterly as his mind strayed to the treatment he received from his superiors daily. He had earned his PhD for god's sake, and they still treated him like an office assistant-slash-janitor.

"Perry, go get me a latte, and don't mess it up like you did last time."

"Perry, the downstairs toilet is clogged, can you get maintenance on it? Or just fix it yourself if you're so smart."

He ground his perfectly straight teeth as the elevator came to a stop. The doors opened with a metallic clank and Perrin was greeted by two surly looking guards.

"What are you doing down here?" The first one approached him, holding out his hand for Perrin's badge. His employer had had the foresight to present him with a physical ID, but the guard's intent examination had Perrin sweating once more. The man looked down at his picture and squinted slightly as he took in Perrin's blue eyes and slightly stooped shoulders. Finally, he seemed to pass the guard's inspection. Perrin had been right to assume that they wouldn't even recognize him, even though he was sure he had seen these guys during their last shift at Genotech.

No one ever sees me, not here anyway. His bitterness returned, stamping out any residual nerves he felt.

"Dr. Carr asked me to grab some of his notes from the Lab. He's in a meeting after lunch and needs to go over them before he talks to the board." He hated using Evan's name like that, the kid was one of the good ones, but just thinking the word 'kid' made him angry. Evan was also an intern and younger than him too, but he got to be down here with the big boys all day. Everyone called him Dr. Carr, no one insulted him by using his first name. Perrin had always been 'Perry' or 'Hey, you, intern!'

Perrin made his way to the Lab and jabbed his thumb into the bio scanner at the door. He chuckled as the name populated with his picture beside it. David Smith stared back at him, Perrin's face plastered onto a fake profile. They had told him his information would revert after the lunch hour was finished and he had no reason to doubt them. The Lab was clean, everything a clinical white, with neatly organized grey, marble counter tops and specimens in cylindrical, covered cases along the edges of each desk. Along the back wall, there was a glass divider, a small area meant to house specimens as they observed behavioral traits during their various experiments. Perrin refused to look back there anymore, not after the last time. He shuddered at the memory of Genotech's first primate trials and shook it off as he walked over to Dr. Jones's desk and opened the case he was working on.

Just need one of these. He reached into his jacket and pulled out a mug they had given him. He unscrewed the base of the mug, as directed. Inside was a compartment he could use to carry the sample they had asked for. He had been told that the cup was lead-lined at the core and would look like a regular thermos during a security check. He carefully picked a sample out of Dr. Jones's case and put it into the mug. As he was closing Jones's case, he heard distant beeping as the bio-scanner activated. He slammed the case shut, struggling as it caught on the edge of the remaining sample before closing properly. He dove over to the nearest desk, yanking his phone from his white coat and grabbing a file off it as he righted himself. He was just quick enough to place the mug on the counter before him before the door opened, letting in one of the guards from earlier.

"You need help finding what you're looking for buddy?" the big guard asked, taking a step into the Lab.

"No! No, I'm fine, I just got caught up sending a text message to Dr. Carr" Perrin casually put the phone in his pocket, his heart jackhammering as he willed it to settle down. Surely this guy could hear it? It was as loud as a drum in his own ears. He turned to the guard as he spoke, "I just need to make sure I'm grabbing the right file, this guy doesn't know the meaning of 'organized'." He pretended to inspect the file in his hands and straightened up, "This looks like it. Wish me luck though, I really don't want to get sent down here on my next break." He shot the guard a charming grin as he made his way to the door. The guard, a younger man with sandy blonde hair and a smile Perrin was sure could make ice melt, grinned back at him.

"I hear ya buddy, sucks being the little guy, doesn't it?" Perrin heard a chuckle escape his lips but saw red at the idea that this man thought of him as a 'little guy'. He tucked the folder under his arm and casually grabbed his coffee mug off the table.

"Yea, tell me about it. I should probably take this for him too, he's a beast without his coffee." The guard nodded and smiled slightly at that. Perrin followed him out of the lab and was escorted down the hall, where the other guard stood at the elevator. He boarded the elevator, careful to duck his head from the camera's view and waved jauntily at them as the doors closed, his blond friend waved back, his grin almost goofy. Once he was alone, Perrin sagged against the wall, always ensuring that his face wasn't visible to the cameras above.

$500,000, wow! He grinned as he looked at the non-descript mug in his hands. *All I need to do is hand this off upstairs!* Life was looking up.

Downstairs in Lab 3, the second sample chamber shattered in its case.

Chapter 1

June 9th, 2027 - Genotech, 16:00

Captain Kara Piers made her way down the brightly lit halls of Genotech, her destination was the largest conference room at the end of the third floor. She had been here only a handful of times; once when her team had first been hired out to the biotechnology firm, and the others for briefings with the head of Genotech's Security Department. She hadn't needed to make other trips in for the past two years, seeing as they were only to be called in under serious circumstances, and there had only been two of those. Open doors and low chatter surrounded her as she made her way down the hall. The lighting above strobed her dark features as she walked briskly, questions abound in her head about what they could possibly have been called in for.

Working for Genotech was a comfortable job, she could admit. Nothing at all like storming a beach or suffering under scorching desert suns, waiting for the next in a stream of never ending battles.

The biotech firm was one of the top three leaders in their industry though and tended to be the target of various, sometimes militant, groups. The big wigs at the top had realized they would need protection.

That's where Piers and her team came in.

They were the problem solvers. They were sent in when the going got tough, and were there to make sure Genotech's threats got going. It was a safe job. A reliable job. She would be the last to say that she preferred this though and her team weren't always particularly happy with their assignments either. Occasionally they had been requested to escort certain shipments to Genotech's various labs across the country. Once, Kara herself had been requested to accompany a group of scientists to Israel for a summit. That had been the most boring week of her life. She had met some interesting characters on that trip though, one who had impressed her specifically, had later joined her team.

Hers wasn't the only solo mission by far, in fact, most of her team regularly took on solo jobs, just for a change from the monotony. Her Second Lieutenant, Ibrahim and one of their Field Medics, John had done just that today, leaving her shorthanded when Lindquist had called her in.

She stirred herself from her thoughts and looked over at the shorter woman accompanying her on this trip into HQ. Cropped, dark hair, a stocky build and large, dark eyes hidden behind rectangular frames, Divya Kaur, her right-hand woman and resident techie, had been requested specifically by Lindquist for this meeting, an anomaly that set her on edge.

She was happy to have the other woman with her. Divya, along with their top Field Medic Anna Parsons, were regular visitors to the Genotech facility. Anna's mentor, Dr. Carla Foreman was the Head of Staff at this facility and Divya often accompanied her on her trips in. It wouldn't look good if she got lost heading into the briefing, not that it would happen, but Divya was a good failsafe just in case.

"It can't be good if they're calling both of us in" Divya said softly as she tapped away at something on her tablet with deep red nails. Kara smiled to herself, the woman wasn't necessarily feminine, but so help anyone that messed with her nails. The Captain snorted in acknowledgement. She may have disliked the monotony of the job, but that didn't mean she wished for an emergency.

In emergencies, people got hurt.

In emergencies, bad things could happen to her team. Yes, they were well trained, but accidents happened. Case and point being exactly why they had been called in.

"Ladies," came a deep voice, as they entered the conference room.

"Ah, Mr. Lindquist, it's been a while," Captain Piers commented lightly as she took the seat nearest her. Lindquist's deep voice matched his looks perfectly. He stood at a lanky 6'5" but possessed the broadest set of shoulders Kara had seen. She had always thought he'd be the perfect football player but she would have been afraid for anyone on the opposite team. Divya sat down across from her, angled towards the Head of the Security Department and waved discreetly at the tiny, red headed woman, Carla, behind him. Lindquist barely acknowledged Kara's cordiality as he put down the folder in his large hands and looked up.

"The meeting will begin once the others arrive."

"Others?" She had been told that this was a private meeting. "What others?"

Lindquist was saved from answering as a small gaggle of scientists entered the room, chattering loudly and occupying the various seats around the oval table. Lindquist gave them a moment to settle in before he cleared his throat, effectively silencing the room.

"We have a problem," he said as he stood up at the head of the table. Tenting his fingers and leaning on the table top, he continued, "I have been informed that as of this morning, the New Candor facility is officially offline." Murmurs broke out around the table as the gathered scientists began to speculate on the nature of the situation. Lindquist cleared his throat lightly again and began moving towards the projector screen behind him. The light of the screen lit up his dark skin in a bluish tint as he approached. A small flick of his fingers and a map of the New Candor division of Genotech appeared on the screen.

"Approximately 6 days ago, there was a major gas leak at the facility." He looked over at Kara, holding her eye for a moment before moving on to Divya whose expression hardened. "We have attempted evacuation procedures, but we are not getting the response that we desire. We have called you all here today for a briefing before we send in our Emergency Response Team. Carla, if you would?" He stepped away from the screen as the stocky woman picked up the dialogue, her accent colouring the words slightly.

"June 3rd, 2027, we received a distress signal from the New Candor facility. The signal was coded Red 22b. In this scenario, all associates are required to assemble in the Bunker of the sub-basement for Quarantine and Containment until the breach is resolved. Considering the size of the lab, the assessment usually takes four days." She looked back at the room from the slide they were viewing. "On the fourth day, NCF is supposed to report back to the home lab to confirm the breach has been resolved. We have not heard from them yet."

More muttering, worried now, from the gathered scientists as Lindquist took his position at the front of the room once again. Kara wondered to herself how important this group was if they couldn't even keep quiet during a briefing and had to rein in the thought, they were only civilians.

"As I said, we have been authorized to send in our Emergency Response Team. I have brought you all together today to bring our ERT Leader up to date on what her team could possibly be dealing with in there. For any of you who don't know yet, this is Kara Piers, Captain of our Emergency Response Team, and Divya Kaur, her Lieutenant and our communications liaison." He motioned towards Kara and Divya, who nodded at the assembled group. "Dr. Milas, can we start with the biotech department?"

A petite, dark skinned woman stood up and started speaking in a surprisingly rich voice. Kara settled herself in, prepared to listen intently.

The next hour was spent listening to theories and speculations about what they would face once they arrived in New Candor. To be perfectly fair, Kara tried her hardest to pay attention to the men and women reporting to her, but a lot of the small details that they deemed important bogged her down. She was also distracted planning the team she would be taking in on this mission. Ibrahim and John were out, of course, but there were a few veterans she knew she would be taking with her.

She was glad that Lindquist had thought to request Divya. The woman was simultaneously taking notes and inputting information into that tablet of hers, occasionally stopping to ask questions and clarifications as she went. As the final doctor sat down, Lindquist stood up, grabbing the attention of the room once again. "I don't believe I need to let any of you know that the subject matter of this meeting is Classified, do I?"

No arguments. There was some shuffling of feet and rustling of coats as some of the gathered doctors avoided Lindquist's sharp gaze.

"Captain," he redirected his gaze to Kara, "Lt. Kaur, could you please join me after the meeting for a few moments? The rest of you are dismissed." Kara and Divya remained seated as the group filed out of the room, noticeably more reserved than when they had arrived.

"The facility has been running on backup generators since the 3rd. It's part of the standard procedure, a failsafe if the leak is a terror strike. Once the alarm has been activated, main power to each level will be cut off, emergency lighting will be active though. All elevators are currently on fire service mode; the operator's key is in here," he said as he approached them with the folder he had been viewing earlier. "In the event that these alarms are triggered, all powered locks are disengaged for quicker evacuation. All except four, that is."

He handed the file to Divya. "The only four that remain active are those in the sub-basement; 'The Bunker', Lab 3 and the roof exit. This is what you will require to deactivate those locks. President Anders has *requested*," he shot a pointed glance at Kara, she could read between the lines, "that you stay out of Lab 3 as you evacuate the building personnel."

"Of course," she replied coolly, as Divya began to inspect the contents of the file. "Anything else we should know?"

"Yes, the generators are only intended to keep powering the buildings for 7 days." He took his seat at the head of the table once more; "this means that the power will cut while you are in the process of evaluating the situation. We will be providing your team with emergency generators for this mission. They're not as strong as the ones at the facility, but they'll give you power to a few key locations. Everything will be prepped and waiting for you to leave tomorrow morning, 06:00."

Hearing the dismissal in his voice, Kara and Divya stood up as one, gathered their possessions and headed towards the doors.

"Ladies," Lindquist's serious voice stopped them at the door, "Be careful. Come home safe."

Before Kara could respond, he swept by them and down the bright hall, leaving behind the faint, woody scent of his aftershave and a bad feeling in the pit of Kara's stomach. Carla squeezed Divya's upper arm reassuringly as she walked past.

"Well that was ominous," Divya muttered as she balanced her notes, the folder and her tablet once again. Kara smiled distractedly as she took the folder from the shorter woman and headed back to the lobby of the building. She felt as if she didn't have all the pieces to this story, and that was never a good feeling before a mission.

Chapter 2

June 9th, 2027 – ERT Training Center, 18:00

"Alright newbie, let's see what you can do," Kara heard a jolly voice as she entered the training gym of their small building.

He's still calling the kid 'newbie'? She thought as she caught sight of them, then realized she was still calling Dean 'the kid' even though he was well into his 30's and he'd been with them for a few months, and smiled.

She could see Cristiano Rodriguez, known as Chris to his friends, and the recruit, Dean Carter in the center of the room, facing off on the mats. Dante Alvarez stood off to the side, watching with vested interest. She had seen the kid sparring with Divya recently, and he lived up to the reputation that had driven her to recruit him so many months ago. She chuckled as she remembered how scared Dean had looked when he thought he had broken one of Divya's nails as he flipped her and pinned her on the blue mats. She leaned against the wall, folder tucked under her arm, and watched the two men as they began to dance.

Though Chris must have outweighed Dean by at least 100lbs, the shorter man didn't seem fazed by this. He took a stance that somewhat resembled the beginnings of a Judo kata, but with looser limbs. Chris, seeming as if he didn't see him as a threat, was in a simple boxing stance, clenched fists brought up to guard his face as he leered over them at the recruit.

That's a mistake, Kara smirked, ready to watch Chris get his ass handed to him. She nodded at Dante, who had glanced over as she settled in and he shook his head in resignation.

Dean's stance seemed so relaxed that even though she expected it, it still surprised Kara when he rushed towards Chris, deftly avoiding the right hook thrown by the larger man. As Chris swung again, Dean grabbed his extended arm with both hands and twisted his body, pivoting on his heel, throwing the man off balance. Taking advantage of this, Dean dropped to the mat and swept out his leg. In seconds, Chris was flat on his back, he jerked to his right to avoid the heel of Dean's foot as it came down at his face and found himself unable to move. Dean had dropped his weight on the larger man, forcing the air from his lungs and straddling his limbs. His thumbs were poised above Chris's eyes, ready to do some serious damage. Chris tapped out and grinned up at the recruit through the hands covering his face. Dean stood up in one fluid motion and offered a hand, grinning back. His dark brown hair was sweaty and sticking to his brown skin in clumps. Chris ran his fingers through his own cropped locks, wiping the sweat back from his brow.

"Not bad kid, not bad at all," he took the offered hand and dusted himself off as he stood, "good job with this one, Cap." He smirked at Kara, pulling the black tank top he had discarded over his broad chest. He was probably the only one on the team that didn't treat her with deference.

"Well, we'll get a chance to see you in action, that's for sure." She forced a smile at Dean, worried after Lindquist's comments at the end of their conversation. "Chris, get the team together in the briefing room, we've got a mission."

Chris seemed stunned, only shaken awake as Kara walked over to Dante to collect her winnings.

"Israel," was all she said to Dante as he handed over the ten bucks he had bet on Chris. Dante shook his head; he should have known better than to bet against her anyway.

"You bet against me Cap?" Chris called after her. Captain Piers raised the ten in a salute to him as she walked towards the conference room.

"Briefing room Chris," was all she said as she shut the door and began preparing for their meeting. She heard the voices of Chris and Dante pass the door and fade away. Glad that they were off to find the rest of the team, she turned her attention to the file before her.

Almost as soon as she finished reading the file, she heard the door open.

Excellent timing as always, she thought as she looked up to see Dean enter the room, followed closely by the rest of her team. Dean, Chris and Dante took the seats facing the front, to her right. Divya and Anna Parsons to her left.

"Divya said we have a mission? Are you shitting me boss?" Chris, eloquent as always. She was nearly as surprised as he was when she had been called into Genotech's HQ. Kara had been on missions at other facilities across the world and some of her team members had joined her on occasion, but this was the first mission on their home turf since the team had come together years ago. Kara leveled her gaze at him as she replied.

"No, I assure you Chris, I am not 'shitting' you."

She looked around at her team, took a deep breath and dove into her briefing.

"I have been informed that we have lost contact with the New Candor Facility as of June 3rd. According to the information Lindquist has shared with us, the facility has been offline for approximately 6 days." She took another breath, observed the stoic expressions of her team and continued. "We have been told that the facility is currently operating under emergency power. Unfortunately, that power is scheduled to shut off around the time of our arrival."

"Of course," Chris. Kara ignored his remark. She had felt the same way when she had heard that bit of information, she just had the good sense to keep her opinion to herself, something Chris was not blessed with.

"We will be provided with our own generators upon arrival, and it is imperative that we set up our base of operations at the nearest lab. Divya?" She looked over at her Lieutenant expectantly.

"Judging by the maps Lindquist provided, the nearest lab is Lab 4, at the South West side of the building's first floor." Divya pulled up the blueprints to the building and sent them over to the screen on the far wall. The image followed the path of the hallway leading out of the main lobby and led them to Lab 4: "when the power goes completely, the elevators will become as useless as paperweights. If we want to use them at all during the evacuation, I suggest we hook them up to their own generator as soon as we land."

"Think you're up for that, Divya?" The Captain asked.

"Yea, it shouldn't be too difficult, if I get some muscle to drag the gennies around, once we find the machine room," she smirked at Chris, who stuck his tongue out at her childishly. Kara didn't mind a few jokes, she understood that jokes were how Chris dealt with stress, and this situation was stressful. There were only a few reasons why New Candor couldn't respond to communications, and none of them were good.

"Alright, so once we get into the building, we secure Lab 4. Chris, Dante, you're with Divya. Divya, can you map out the route to the machine room on that tablet of yours?" Divya smiled and tapped something out on her screen.

"Done," she said after a few seconds, "I've sent maps of the building's main systems to the team's handhelds as well, just in case."

"Good thinking," Kara nodded, she didn't say anything else out loud, but she didn't need to, they all knew that spreading out their assets was always a good idea.

"Once our base of operations is secured, our next step is surveillance. Lindquist has also included the passcodes to the CCTV system in here Divya," she passed the papers off to Divya as she spoke, "we'll need eyes everywhere, so you'll need to set this up when we get in, preferably before the machine room."

"Agreed," Divya chimed in, "it's better to know what we're dealing with before we head up there anyway." She made a few notes on her tablet and handed the papers back to Kara.

"Chris," Kara looked over to him as she spoke.

"Yea boss?" he replied with forced cheer.

"Once you secure the machine room with Divya, you and Dante report back to me. I'll need those muscles to drag a few more generators down to the sub-basement," she caught Dante's eye and acknowledged his nod with her own. "Dean, you and Anna are with me until the unit is together. Once we've regrouped, Divya, you take mission command and the rest of you get those gennies down to the sub-basement."

She took a moment for the plan to sink in.

"Any questions?" She asked, looking around at her team. No one came forward, "No? Good, we all have our parts to play. There are civilians in there, they need us to be organized and calm to get them out of there. If we encounter any sort of terror threat or enemy, the priority is the people. We're not authorizing deadly fire until we assess the situation. Divya, that's up to you."

Divya paled slightly and Anna clasped her shoulder reassuringly. Kara knew she had been on missions like this before, Divya had been by her side for half of her career in fact. It was the reason she asked her to be a part of the team, and Divya had accepted, coming on as Kara's Lieutenant before Chris had joined them. Divya always reacted like this when they acknowledged the importance of her success though. It wasn't easy being the eyes and ears of a mission, especially when they were quite literally, going in dark.

"If there are no questions, we meet tomorrow, 06:00 at The Bus," her team smiled at the nickname, "dismissed."

They all rose from their seats and herded out the door.

"The Bus? What's that?" She heard Dean ask Dante.

"Oh, you wouldn't know what that is, would you?" Dean shook his head. He had only been with the team for a few months, so Kara wasn't surprised that he hadn't caught on to their jokes just yet.

Dante stopped beside the younger man to explain. "It's all Divya's fault, she said that the Humvee looked like something out of that kid detective cartoon. You know, with the talking dogs and the guy that's always hungry?"

"Oh, yea, Mystery Gang?" Dean asked. Kara looked at him out of the corner of her eye, smiling at his eagerness. The tips of Dean's ears went red when he realized she had heard them. "Uh, my brother used to watch it when he was younger."

Dante chuckled at his embarrassment. "It's okay dude, we've all watched it, especially after Div coined the nickname for us."

Dean smiled and ruffled the hair at the back of his head as Dante mentioned Divya again.

Hmm, that's not good, Kara thought as she walked past them, heading to her room to pack for the mission.

She reached her rooms quickly, got her travel rucksack and started rifling through her drawers for everything she needed. Not even ten minutes into her packing, there was a knock at her door.

"Come in Chris," she called out, already knowing who it was.

"It's like you expect this Kara," Chris said as he walked into her room, "It's not like—"

"Like you do this before every mission we've had together in the last 6 years? No, not at all," she interrupted him, folding her clothes small enough to leave space for her Ruger in the pack.

"I thought we weren't using deadly force?" He smirked as he watched her holding the Ruger, almost lovingly, before depositing it into her pack.

"It's more of a good luck charm than anything."

The gun had been given to her by her father before she had left home on her first term of active duty. He had hidden it from her mother and snuck it to her just before she had left home. It was the last time she had seen him happy, excited to see her off and proud. When she had seen him next, he hadn't woken up to greet her. She hadn't seen his smile in a long time.

"Cap," Chris said gently, rousing her from her memories, "you okay?"

"Yea, I'm fine Chris, so, the usual?" She asked, turning around to grab the bottle of Glenlivet she knew he was here for. Chris smiled at her, a genuine one now, nothing forced when it came to this little ritual.

"You know it!"

Kara smiled in return and grabbed the two whiskey glasses she kept in her cabinet. She poured out a decent shot of the single malt and offered a glass to Chris. "To a successful mission."

Chris raised his glass to her, the tinkling of glass touching followed, then they both knocked back the shot. There was a quick, smooth burn, followed by a soft heat blooming in her belly as the alcohol settled her nerves.

"You think they're telling us everything?" Chris asked quietly as he set his glass down and leaned against her desk.

She sighed and closed the flap on her rucksack.

"Do they ever?" She ran her hand down her face, tugging at her chin slightly, before letting go. "I don't think either of us have ever had a full disclosure mission."

Chris grunted a short laugh.

"You got a point there, Cap," he stood up and stretched, as if he had been in that position for hours rather than seconds. "Well, maybe we're just too suspicious for our own good?"

Kara doubted it, and she knew Chris doubted it as well, but she gave him a small smile. This was all part of the ritual, reassurance. Chris accepted her small comfort and headed out the door.

"Chris," she stopped him before he walked out, "Keep an eye out for Dean, would you?" She didn't know why she asked, she didn't need Chris distracted trying to babysit the kid. Chris seemed to understand though.

"Keep an eye out? He kicked my ass earlier, didn't you notice?" He laughed and she felt some of her tension bleed away. She smiled.

"I did, actually, or the ten bucks in my pocket noticed at least." Chris tried his best not to laugh again as he looked mock offended. Kara chuckled and shut the door on him. She stripped, headed into her shower and stood under the hot water, trying to relax. It was always like this. Chris had known her long enough to know she needed to unwind before the stress got to her. Stress led to mistakes and they didn't need any of those before the mission even began. She felt her tension melt away as the water rolled off her body. Ten minutes later, she emerged from the bathroom, threw on a large t-shirt and settled into bed with her remote. She was expected at the garage earlier than the rest of the team. She threw on the game show channel and fell asleep to the soothing sounds of 'What's My Name Again'.

Chapter 3

05:00 came around sooner than she had liked and she found herself overseeing the last hour of prep as her team assembled at The Bus. Kara was checking the status of their M14 EBR's as Chris joined the others at the bus. The EBR's had been Lindquist most recent purchase for their team, they weren't exactly allowed to have the most recent army model but these worked beautifully. Kara cocked the rifle and checked the scope, being careful not to sight anyone. She was overly careful when it came to gun safety.

Chris made himself known as Dean hoisted himself into the back of the Humvee.

"Come on newbie, you're holding us up," his voice rang out and bounced off the domed ceiling of the garage and he chuckled as he nudged Dean over the lip of the door. Kara looked up as she packed the rifle away and saw Dean stumble slightly, blush and grin when

Divya giggled. He settled himself at the far end of the compartment.

"Don't mind him," Dante said, clapping him on the shoulder, "he's like a kid with candy whenever he has a mission."

"Gotta put this energy to use somehow, Dante!" Chris shouted as he hauled a large pack into the small space with him. He sat down beside Divya and slung his arm across her shoulder. "So Div, you ready to put this muscle to use?" He winked lecherously over at Dean, who rolled his eyes and raised an eyebrow at Divya. Divya shifted slightly to free one arm, reached up and pinched the soft skin of Chris's upper arm, hard.

The larger man yelped and withdrew his arm from around her shoulders, "Alright, alright, I get it," he sulked, moving over to give her more personal space. He belatedly shrugged on the jacket he had laid across his lap, watching her with mock accusation as he pulled it on.

"Thank you," was her quiet reply as she focused her attention on the tablet before her. Kara watched the scene with a small, amused smile on her face as she directed the last few packages to the correct areas.

The only one who wouldn't be joining them on the drive into New Candor was Anna. Anna would meet them with the generators once they arrived. She needed to bring in the emergency med supplies with her, just to be safe. They were sure the supplies wouldn't make an 8-hour trip in the Humvee. Hell, she wouldn't be surprised if her whole team melted on the way there themselves. No, it was much safer for Anna to bring the supplies in on the half hour helicopter ride. She hopped into the back of The Bus as the Genotech employees loaded the last few boxes into the other vehicles for them.

"Alright team, listen up," she started, buckling herself into one of the empty seats in the back. "8 hours until we reach Ground Zero. Divya, you can take the time to familiarize yourself with those blueprints, I want you to be able to lead us blind if you need to."

Divya nodded. She was most likely already able to do that, but Kara knew she would keep at it until they arrived anyway. "Dante, run through the plan with Dean, I want him able to recite it back to me whenever I ask, backwards if I want it." Dante nodded and clapped Dean on the shoulder again. This would be his first real mission with the team, and Kara needed to know she could count on him.

"Looks like you're mine for the day kid," Dante smiled grimly. Dean spared him a small nod as Chris opened his mouth to comment.

"Rodriguez." Kara snapped, causing the large man to shut his mouth.

"Yea Boss?" Chris looked at her quizzically, she didn't normally give him instructions like this prior to a mission.

"Shut up. We have 8 hours in this thing, if you disturb what little sleep I manage to get, I WILL throw you out the back of it." She held his gaze, unsmiling as he grinned at her.

"Alright, jeez, no one appreciates the muscle." He grumbled, still grinning as he leaned back folded his arms across his chest and closed his eyes.

§

"Shh, don't let your mom see it, but I felt like I needed to get you something special," her father's voice, "It's legal, fully licensed, what do you think?" Why couldn't she see him? She looked around but everything was black. Kara lifted her hands to her face and felt something like a shroud. She tore at it until it came away and looked down at her hands. Blood? Why was there so much blood?

"Kara Piers, reporting for duty," she heard her own voice, years younger. She looked around once again. The city around her was in flames, corpses staring back at her from burning vehicles, mouths gaping open in silent screams. She backed up and tripped on something. She fell. The body she had tripped over began crawling over to her, leaving a bloody trail behind it. It was Chris.

"Cap, Captain," Chris croaked as he grabbed for her throat, "Captain!"

She struggled, lashing out at the corpse that held her.

"Woah, calm down Cap, it's just a dream," Chris held her shoulders, gently pushing her back into the seat so she couldn't attack him. The Bus had come to a stop. Her team stood around the cramped, dimly lit compartment checking their weapons and ammunition, ignoring their interaction. Her nightmares were no secret to the team, each of them had been on overnight missions with her before and she trusted them not to ask. Chris was the only one who knew what they were about.

"I'm fine," she ground out, jaw clenched, "has Anna arrived yet?"

Chris released her shoulders and stepped back as she unlatched her seatbelt and neatened herself up. "She radioed in a few minutes ago, there was some interference in her communication, but they're almost here with the generators. The Genotech guys just dropped off the last Humvee and ducked out. We're at the New Candor city limits."

"Dean, Dante, you're in Bus 1. Divya, you're with me here. Chris, when Anna arrives she's with you in Bus 3." She shook off the dream and took charge. "Once they drop the gennies, Dean, Dante, Chris you're responsible for loading them into the Humvees." She heard the whirr of approaching helicopter blades as she exited the back of the Humvee. Dust kicked up and she shielded her eyes as the bird touched down. When the dust settled Kara darted under the rotors and helped Anna unload the MediKit.

Lindquist had sent the strongest members of his team with her and the gennies were unloaded almost as soon as they had landed. With Dante's help they loaded the large pieces of machinery into the Humvees while Anna and Divya checked the status of the MediKit. Kara watched as the last of Darcy's men closed the canvas flaps at the back of the last Humvee and rapped on the metal.

"We're all done here ma'am," he said, his accent thick and foreign, "Good luck in there." Kara nodded at his statement and motioned for her team to get moving as the men hopped back into the helicopter and kicked up more dust.

Her team split up and she got behind the wheel of the nearest Humvee, Divya hopped into the seat beside her. Kara grabbed the ComBox on the dash and depressed the button.

"Alright folks, follow me and try not to jostle the merchandise too much," she said with a smile trying to brush off the remark of Darcy's man and the remnants of her dream that still clung to her, like cobwebs. She turned to Divya and motioned to the tablet in her hands, "Lead the way."

The city life thrived as it did any other night. New Candor was a midsized city and Kara took it in as the lights from the streets flashed across their faces. She could smell street food cooking and realized she hadn't eaten anything since they had left the garage. Her stomach growled at the thought of food and she felt something land in her lap. She looked down at the next set of lights and saw a granola bar in her lap.

"It's not much but I figure it's the best we can get right now," Divya smiled at her. Kara could see some of the tension in the set of her eyes but right now they were just hungry.

"Thanks," She said as she tore the wrapper and bit into the bar. It wasn't bad, one of the strawberry ones she liked. Divya held her bar up in a mock salute before tearing into it herself.

City streets became bare, the bustling crowds thinning out. Kara wondered how people could just go about their lives as normal when Genotech could possible be hijacked right now and realized that these people had no idea what was happening in their own town.

Street lights were few and far between now. They were surrounded on both sides by forest and Kara realized they were heading to the outskirts of town. The occasional streetlight flashed overhead, throwing Divya's thick features into harsh shadows.

Kara drove on.

Minutes later they arrived at a tall, fenced in building in an industrial area tucked into the mountainside, almost at the edge of the city. The other buildings around it seemed unoccupied.

"Genotech owns everything on this lot," Divya explained, seemingly knowing what she was thinking. "Their team prefers less interactions with the public, hence the location. Those buildings off to the side out of commission right now. The main building in the center is the one we want." She pointed to the large, dark office building that was dwarfed by the mountain behind it, despite its height. Divya typed something into her tablet and the white gate before them rolled smoothly open on its own.

"Well, looks like we've got a bit of power to work with right now," Divya said, pushing her glasses up the bridge of her nose. Her dark eyes were calculating as she surveyed the buildings before them. Kara could see her trying to take steady breaths, but she didn't seem any calmer for them.

"Alright Div, let's get that garage open before we move," She said before speaking over the CB to the rest of the team.

"Team, once those doors are open, we're making a straight shot for the garage." A chorus of affirmatives later and she signalled to Divya to open the doors. They watched them grind open slowly, screeching occasionally and waited for any movement, attacks or any sign of life at all. It was too quiet. Kara put the Humvee into drive and made a line for the garage doors as they opened fully. She followed the white arrows and ramps down until they were at the lowest level of the garage.

There were still lights down here.

She shut off the vehicle and jumped out, Divya following quickly after. The rest of her team dismounted and spread out, weapons drawn, tactical lights scoping out the darkness of the garage.

"All clear," came Dean's voice from the back of the last Humvee.

"Clear," Chris, as he swept the shadows at the far end of the garage.

"Clear," Dante from the other side of the vehicles.

"Clear!" Anna from the shadows on the opposite end, "What's that stink?" She wrinkled her nose as her light swept the wall, coming to rest on the half full dumpster.

"Well, no one's been authorized to be here for 6 days now Anna, what did you expect?" Came Chris's voice as he holstered his weapon and sauntered back to the group. Divya smiled and slung her arm around Anna's shoulders, pulling her in for a moment before Kara got them back to business.

"Alright, let's make as much use of the remaining power as we can," Kara said as she popped open the back hatch of the Humvee, "Chris, Dante, Dean, get to it. Divya, you have a job to do. Anna, with me."

Between the five of them, they maneuvered the generators nearer to the large loading doors. Anna doubled back for the MediKit as Chris propped the door open with a heavy weight from the back of one of the Humvees. The delivery elevators opened when Kara held down the button.

"Well at least that works," Kara said as the elevator doors dinged open and they returned to the task of getting the generators to where they needed them. Kara kept looking around, expecting someone to react to their presence. They weren't being very quiet and they should have drawn attention at this point. She ground her teeth as they dragged the last generator across the lip of the elevator door.

"What if the power shuts off while we're in here?" whispered Chris loudly as the doors shut, leaving them in dim light.

"Then you get to climb out of that little door up there and lug these out on your own," Kara replied smoothly, shutting him up. He had nothing to worry about though, as the doors opened to reveal the empty lobby, and let in the soft lights from the hallway.

"It's so quiet," Anna muttered as she grabbed her end of the generator, "it just doesn't feel right."

She was right, the backup lights in low power mode made for eerie, yellowish, lighting down the halls. Kara tried to peer further down the hall before them, but the lights were so dim that she felt strained.

There were no sounds.

She could hear the slight hum of overworked lights sure, but there was nothing else, it was as if the entire building was holding its breath. Waiting for whatever would happen next. Kara shook her head to clear the thoughts and radioed down to Divya, "Div, what are we looking at here?"

"Nothing Captain, there's nothing going on. I've got all of the cameras up and I haven't seen a single soul." She sounded slightly worried. Kara didn't blame her, if the employees weren't being held hostage, what would keep them from checking in for two days?

"Alright, we're waiting, get your butt up here soldier," she grunted as they hauled the last generator out of the elevator. She heard the whirring of machinery as the passenger elevator across the room came to life.

"On my way."

Minutes later the team was gathered in Lab 4, minus two members. Chris and Dante had headed up to the electrical room to hook up the first of the three generators they would need. Kara swept the room with her gaze. Everything seemed slightly off. Nothing she didn't expect, just signs of people who had been required to leave in a hurry. Over on one table a half full cup of coffee sat moldering, its contents more gelatinous than liquid.

"We're all set here Cap," Chris's voice crackled over her radio. "Heading back up now."

"Roger that Chris," she replied as she nosed around in a stack of papers left out on a lab desk. "Anything out of place?"

"Nothing Cap, this place–deserted." She could feel the unease in his voice. She couldn't blame him.

"What's with the interference Divya?" she asked, turning to her Lieutenant.

"There's an electrical storm moving in Captain," Divya replied, sounding slightly worried. "Just a bad time for a mission, that's all."

"Will it interfere with the generators?"

"No, we should be fine." She paused, "Captain, some of these codes don't work." She had been trying to access the remaining CCTV cameras, those in the sub-basement.

"What?" She snapped, there was no way Lindquist had given them faulty information.

"Yea, it seems that the codes that headquarters has were changed the day of the leak." Divya was typing and staring at the screen before her as she spoke. "Just regular changes to the passcode, done every three months or so. The codes Lindquist gave us were before they were changed and no one's been able to report the new ones to HQ."

"Can you figure it out?" She asked and waited patiently as Divya checked. Minutes went by before she answered.

"Ok, yea, I can figure this out, just needs a little bit of work on my part but we should be in soon," Divya said distractedly as she continued typing. Not wanting to disturb her, Kara walked over to Dean and Anna who had already returned from stringing lights along the path to the elevator. The trio was busy setting up floodlights around the room as Chris and Dante returned.

"How is it out there?" Kara asked them as they moved to help with the setup.

"Quiet as ever," Chris replied, unwinding a thick reel of grey cable behind him. "Dante says he heard something moving around, but I couldn't hear anything when we stopped. I think the atmosphere is getting to him." Kara acknowledged this information with a nod and turned to Dante.

"Alright let's get the elevators set, Div is busy. Dante, you have those directions to the machine room?" Dante nodded as he pulled out his handheld. "Good, take Dean with you and head up there, we need to secure that shaft with what time we have left. Let me know if you see anything while you're up there." Dean and Dante grabbed the second generator and headed out the door.

"What's wrong?" Asked Chris. He knew she wouldn't normally deviate from the plan. Kara left Anna to finish the setup of the floodlights and stepped aside with Chris.

"Just a little wrench," she said, hoping it would be the only one. "Lindquist has the wrong codes for the cameras in the sub-basement."

"We're going in blind?" Chris exclaimed, as softly as he could, fidgeting with the cuff of his thick gloves.

"Not with Divya here, she's working it out right now. Just be ready to go when she gives us the word," she assured him before crossing the lab to check in with Divya.

"Any luck?" She asked, placing her hand on the back of the chair Divya occupied.

"Yea, I'm getting there, just scanning the IP range right now," she muttered as she opened another tab on the screen that requested a username and password, "Ok, let's see admin and…"

The screen opened, showing the shadowy sub-basement hallway. "Excellent job soldier!" Kara exclaimed, relief coursing through her body at not having to do a blind sweep downstairs.

"I can't believe they just switched to one of the default passwords," Divya muttered again, shaking her head in disbelief. "This is why they should change it to something harder, do you see how easy it was for me to get in there?!"

It didn't seem that easy to Kara, but instead of saying that, she simply clapped Divya on the shoulder and left her to view the tapes.

"Captain," she heard Dean's voice over the radio, "got the—set up—heading—soon."

"Dean, you're breaking up," she pressed the button called into her radio. This storm was going to be a pain if they needed to call in medical aid.

"—on our way—" Well, she could understand that, she signalled to Chris who walked over and grabbed his end of the last generator. Anna threw a headlamp at her, which she caught and secured in place, just in case. No sooner had she done that when the power cut.

"Well, shit," was all she heard in the dark. She'd give one guess to who that came from. After a few seconds in the dark, there was a humming in the room and the lights Anna had been working on glowed to life.

"Well, at least we know they work," Anna said, smiling and obviously proud that she had set them up correctly. Chris looked at her with incredulity.

"You mean you didn't know what you were doing?!" Anna laughed and shrugged, grabbing her weapon and one of the packs off the floor in front of her. Divya looked back from the screen and grinned at her.

"Hey! They work!" Came a surprised voice from the door to the lab. Chris turned his incredulous look to Dean.

"You chose the newbie and the medic to set up floodlights and you're surprised they don't know what they're doing? Doesn't Ibrahim usually do this stuff?" Dean asked as he strolled in and grabbed another pack from the floor. Chris looked over at Kara, who shrugged and smiled.

"They figured it out" was all she said as she grabbed her end of the generator and turned to Divya.

"Divya, we've got a portable ComBox with us, the storm shouldn't interfere with that, should it?" Divya shook her head.

"The internal ComBox communicates above 30MHz, so we should be fine within the building," Divya mused. "We should definitely expect some interference with the walkies and the external though. Our handhelds should be working fine for the moment, but I think at the peak of it we won't be getting much out of them if we need them, other than the stored data in there."

"When do you anticipate it to peak?" Kara asked, releasing the genny to adjust her gloves and holster.

"In about an hour maybe two if we're lucky." Divya brought up a few weather maps on the console in front of her. The green grid of radar lit up the dim room, "Looks like it'll last most of the night as well, but that won't stop me from getting into that feed."

"Good, once you get a camera in that Bunker, let me know, we'll go from there." She motioned to the rest of the team, "let's get down to the basement." They headed out.

Chapter 4

June 10th, 2027 – New Candor Genotech, 17:00

Divya watched the team leave the lab and turned to find them on the cameras before her. She wasn't too concerned to be left alone; from what she had seen, there was nothing in this building to be afraid of.

"Alright, let's see what we've got here," she said to no one as she pulled up the footage from the last week and found the feed for the Bunker. She watched as the crew on the screen responded to the alarm and shuffled down the stairwells to the sub-basement. This is what she needed. She radioed down to the Captain.

"Kara, I've got it." She waited for a response, and when none came she pressed the button again, "Kara, can you read me?"

"Div—hear you—" She didn't know if Kara was saying 'I can't hear you' or 'I hear you'. Divya shook her head derisively, this storm was going to be annoying.

"I'm in the security footage for the Bunker Captain, I should be able to get into the live feed from here; I'll radio when I'm in." Nothing from Kara. Divya could only assume she had gotten the message. She tore into another granola bar and slowed the feed to watch as a few of the employees were inspected before they were permitted to enter the Bunker. She left it up on the screen as she began trying to break into the live footage, chewing on the granola bar hands free as she typed. Out of the corner of her eye she saw when the doors to Lab 3 opened, allowing someone to stumble out. She turned her full attention to the footage and she could see something that seemed like mist rolling out of the door behind the figure. She leaned towards the screen, watching in horror as the orderly proceedings before her turned to full blown panic as people rushed to get away from the rolling mist.

Security procedures forgotten, the lab crews surged into the Bunker, some needing to be dragged in. Within minutes, the only ones left outside the doors were laying on the floor, dead, she was sure. The light mist rolled over the figures, dissipating slowly. She paused the feed and leaned back in her seat, pulling the forgotten granola bar from her lips. Scrubbing her face with her palm, she tried to get the image of screaming faces out of her mind. Something tickled at the back of her mind as she walked over to the ComBox and picked up the mic.

"Captain," she spoke softly, still affected by what she had seen, "are you set up yet?"

"What is it Divya?" Kara's voice came roughly over the radio. "Did you break into the feed?" Divya closed her eyes and asked.

"Not yet, I just watched the footage from last week, how bad is it down there?"

"It's fine, Chris is stumbling like a fool in the dark, that's all," Kara replied. Divya could hear Chris protesting in the background, "I assume you didn't call to make small talk, soldier."

How could Kara say that it wasn't bad? She had seen the bodies, no one else had been here for six days; it had to smell horrible down there. That same feeling scratched at the back of her mind now.

"What about the bodies?" She asked, gears working as she stared at the frozen image on the screen.

"Bodies? What bodies? Divya, if you're afraid of the dark—"

Divya stretched the mic over to the desk as Kara spoke. She pressed the forward button and watched as the bodies twitched and pushed themselves up. The hallway had been clear when they had gotten into the camera feed, before the power cut, that's what was so unsettling. Divya pressed play as the first one got to its feet and watched as it lumbered slowly off the screen, out of view of the security camera.

"Divya? DIVYA?" Kara's voice came from the speaker.

"We have a problem."

Kara paused, catching the tension in her voice, "Dean, Dante draw your weapons. Anna, help Chris fix those lights," Kara snapped out to the team, "I'm on my way up."

Divya placed the mic back on the cradle and grabbed her weapon from beside the desk. She hooked the strap over her shoulder and checked the safety. She walked over to the lab door, locked it manually, and returned to the screen. Kara would want as much information as she could get.

§

Kara, weapon drawn, made her way to the elevator as Dean and Dante readied their weapons; she nodded to them as she passed. Whatever she had read from Divya's voice wasn't good and she needed to know what was going on. Why had Divya mentioned bodies? She pressed the button for the lobby and the elevator hummed to life, lights a bit dimmer than when they had first arrived. It was a little different going up without Chris's incessant chatter to keep the silence out.

As the chrome doors opened, she stepped out and swept across the lobby with her tactical light, taking more care in the shadows outside the ring of lights they had strung along the hall. Slowly, she made her way down the hall toward Lab 4, noticing the complete lack of sound, so different from their initial entrance. Now, there was no hum of fluorescent lights, no whirr of A/C, nothing that she associated with a large building like this. It was unnerving, but helpful; if anyone made a sound, she'd be sure to hear them. She shook her head. Divya's tone was getting to her, making her jump at shadows. She reached the clean lab doors and peeked through the window, she could see the shorter woman crouching over the computer as she had left her earlier. Kara rapped her fist against the glass, startling Divya, who turned towards the door, weapon raised. She let it drop to her side when she recognized Kara and rushed to let her in.

"We have trouble," she stammered before Kara could even say anything. She had never seen Divya look so frantic, there were strands of hair escaping her tight ponytail and crumbs around her lips, "I needed to know where it came from, so I checked on the feed from Lab 3 as well," she chattered as she led the Captain over to the screen and pushed her down into the seat.

"Div, what—" Kara spluttered as she was forced to sit down. Divya reached past her and pressed play. The screens showed a line of employees waiting to get into the Bunker. As she watched, the scene unfolded before her eyes, "Oh god."

"That's not all," Divya changed the camera on the screen to show a lab. "This is Lab 3, in the sub-basement." She gave Kara a look that asked for her permission. Kara nodded and looked at the screen again.

There were people in the lab. She could see them clearly. She remembered Lindquist telling them that Lab 3 and the Bunker were run on their own generators and put it out of her mind. Something was wrong with them. As she watched, she noticed more things that set her nerves on edge. The figure at the lab desk closest to the camera reached out for a pen.

"Why are they moving so slowly?" She voiced. Divya just nodded as they continued to watch. The scientist picked up the pen with loose fingers and lifted it. The pen slipped from his fingers and clattered onto the desk below. Kara could almost hear the sound it made. The scientist was not distracted by this though, he simply continued the motion, writing something in the space before him and returning the 'pen' to where he had picked it up. Everyone in the room moved as if they were standing in molasses, "What the hell is this?" She asked, horrified, and not understanding why.

The mechanical behaviour of the men in the room was unnatural, they moved like theme park attractions and was that blood on the coat of one of them? Looking harder, Kara saw that there was blood on the desks too, and what looked like a body in the back corner of the room.

"I don't know," Divya said worriedly, "I think we're safe from them, they're locked in there by biometrics and they haven't tried to escape all week. I checked."

Kara couldn't tear her eyes away as she watched one of the men in the back of the room walk into a glass partition. She could see a bloody mark on the glass where he had hit his head hard enough to break skin. He rebounded slightly and tried to walk through the glass once more. Something about the hopeless repetition sent a shiver down her spine. She swallowed the fear that tried to creep in and pushed back from the desk abruptly.

"We need eyes inside that Bunker," she said to Divya as she stalked over to the ComBox.

Depressing the button for the mic, she spoke to Rodriguez. "Chris, can you hear me?"

After a few long seconds, she heard the static of the radio, "Loud and clear Captain." She wasn't sure when she'd been so relieved to hear Chris's voice, "What's going—" He was cut off by a loud clanging noise, "Jesus Christ!"

"What was that?!" She was on edge after seeing the video feed, her eyes kept darting to the desk, watching Divya work.

"Ah, nothing Chief, Dante just dropped one of the flood lamps."

"Captain…"

"Tell Dante to be more careful, we can't afford to lose any of those lights," she ordered. Away from the screen, she felt more in control of the situation.

"Yea, you got it Cap. Dante! Cap says smarten up!" She heard Dante grumble something that made Chris laugh.

"Captain, we have movement," came Divya's voice from behind her. She stretched the cable of the mic and peered over at the screen. The same scientist from before had turned toward the laboratory doors and was making his way toward it slowly. As they watched, he raised his right hand to the biometric scanner.

"Chris, weapons trained on the lab hallway. NOW!" She commanded forcefully. She released the mic, "I need to see that hallway Divya."

Divya changed the camera view to the hall. They could see the team, weapons trained down the hall, with Chris edging down the hall. Kara could practically hear the hiss of the doors as they opened, letting the man out into the hallway.

§

Chris had been feeling uneasy since the night before. He was used to pre-mission jitters but something about this whole ordeal had felt off from the minute Kara had been called into Genotech. Hearing Kara's voice across the radio now, he knew something was up. The Captain sounded like she was barely restraining a full panic.

"Cap says smarten up!" He called out to Dante, hoping to cut the tension he could sense rolling out of the radio speakers. He rapped his bare knuckles off his temple and pointed in Dante's direction, he had taken his thick gloves off to help set up the cables they had brought down.

"If I smarten up, that'll make you the only idiot left in the group Chris," Dante mumbled as he picked up the light he had dropped. Kara's tone changed immediately in her next communique.

"Weapons trained on the lab hallway. NOW!"
He dropped the mic and readied his weapon,
flicking off the safety as he swung the muzzle
towards the lab hall. In the corners of his vision,
he could see the rest of the team mimicking his
actions, just as the doors down the hall hissed
open.

After a few moments of waiting that had Chris
beginning to edge towards the open hall,
someone appeared at the mouth of the hallway.
It was a man. He looked like he was a bit lost and
injured, judging by the slow gait. Chris made a
slow approach, not wanting to startle him.

"Easy there, we're here to help." He took
another slow step forward and motioned to the
others to drop their muzzles. "We're the
Emergency Response Team, sent out by Darcy
Lindquist." He wasn't sure if this guy even
knew the head of security, but better to keep
talking in that calm voice, it always worked on
civilians. He took another slow step forward and
the guy raised his head to look at him. The man
twitched.

What's up with this guy? He thought to himself as he saw the man's face highlighted by the harsh light. It looked like someone had clawed at him sometime within the last week. There were oozing, red gouges running down each side of his face, and his eyes were clouded over with cataracts. Chris felt a shiver run up his spine. Something was very, very wrong with this guy. He backed up, bringing his weapon up quickly. At the sudden movement, the scientist's eyes cleared and focussed straight on him. In seconds, the man was on him, fingers distorted into claws and teeth bared as he snapped at Chris's throat. He brought his arm up between them, unintentionally lodging the meaty part of his bare palm between the man's teeth. One sharp pain later and the man was forcibly pulled from him, a chunk of Rodriguez between his gnawing teeth.

He looked past the crazed man and saw Dean struggling with him, weapon wrapped around the scientist's throat like a makeshift garrote.

The man was larger than Dean and Dean backed up, trying to keep him under control. As Chris watched, Dean backed down the hall and into the lab through the open door. He heard the growls of other things in the room and dashed towards the door to pull Dean out. He made it to the doorway and watched as Dean slammed the hand of the scientist he held into the scanner on the wall.

"NO!" Chris shouted, slamming his good fist on the door, "DEAN!" He couldn't hear anything from beyond. Leaning his forehead on the door he punched again, weakly this time. Kara had asked him to keep an eye on the kid.

§

"Lab 3!" Before she had finished the words, Divya had the lab on the screen. They watched Dean struggle with the man he held as the others in the room clambered towards him. He shoved the scientist into the oncoming crowd and dove under the closest lab desk, probably meaning to come back out with his weapon ready. Almost as soon as he had disappeared, everything on the screen stilled. Each rabid man calmed and turned back to his never-ending tasks.

"I need a speaker in that room Divya," Divya nodded and opened another screen.

"Got it!" She thrust a headset into Kara's hands.

"Dean! Don't move!" She heard her voice echoing throughout the building. Divya had sent Dean's screen to the large projector against one wall of the room. On the small screen, Kara could see Chris raise his head at the sound of her voice. He looked over at the security camera, she could almost read the hope on his face.

"I need you to put your hand out slowly so I know you can hear me, soldier." She hoped she wasn't sending him to his death with this one small gesture, but she needed to know she had a line of contact. She didn't want to risk the radio, there was still interference, and that might help them pinpoint his location. She watched the screen intently as slowly, so slowly, Dean stuck his arm out from beneath the desk, thumb up to the camera. She sighed as he withdrew the arm, bringing no attention to himself as he did it.

So, it's movement, she thought as she watched the scientists milling about the room, her mind snapped back to Chris's slow approach and the moment the man turned violent. *Rapid movement, at least.*

She took a breath and spoke into the headset again.

"Alright, listen up team. We've got a whole new situation here, we've got an asset trapped in that lab with them and no way to get in without risking him." She looked over at the screen showing the hallway, then back at Dean. "As far as I can tell, these things are attracted to fast movement, Dean. If you leave that spot or move too quickly, they'll be on you faster than stink on a pig. Seeing as we can't locate a safe exit for you,

you'll just have to stay still for now and shut off your walkie. We don't know how much noise will attract them and we don't want them homing in on you because you need to hear my pretty voice, you got that kid?" Another slow and deliberate thumbs up.

What the hell is this kid made of? She didn't know many recruits that could handle this kind of situation so well and made a note to thank Darcy for sending her to Israel when they got out of this hell hole. She continued.

"The rest of you; these things seem to hear and react to certain noises. They're not reacting to this announcement right now and I think that's because it's normal to listen to announcements for them. I'm sure the alarms have been blaring during the past week. If we make any more sudden noises like earlier, *DANTE*, it'll bring them out." She watched as Dante hung his head. He didn't need chastising, but she needed her team to be on point from here on out if they were going to get Dean out of there.

Kara handed the headset back to Divya and walked over to the ComBox. "Chris, has Anna patched you up yet?" She watched him make his way over to the CB, Anna hovering around him as he responded.

"She's working on it Cap, sucker got me good." She could hear the wince of pain as Anna pressed a sore spot on his hand.

"Alright, whatever this is, we don't know if it's communicable. You need to get your ass up here and into containment. Now."

He saluted into the camera awkwardly, with his good hand, and struggled to get up. Anna's voice came on the line: "We'll get him up there as soon as he's patched Captain, I'll make sure of it." Kara just nodded to herself, not needing to affirm that. She walked back to Divya and spoke into the headset once more.

"Dean, once we have Chris patched, we're going to pull them outside, don't make a move until then." Another thumbs up, not even a shake this time.

They viewed the hallway camera as Anna patched Chris up; Divya excused herself to set up a small quarantine at the back of the lab they were occupying. She'd had the foresight to choose a lab with a small glass room and a gurney at the back, thinking Anna might need it for any medical emergencies. She hadn't thought too much about it before, but Divya hated to think of what this room had been used for, now that she knew what existed in this building. The team arrived as Divya finished clearing the room. Chris was being held up between Anna and Dante, his wound bleeding through the bandage already.

"Cap, I feel fine."

"That's not a chance I'm willing to take soldier," she said as she took Anna's place under his left arm, freeing the woman up to make sure her patient was comfortable. "We have no idea what we're dealing with. Divya will go through the feed and maybe we'll learn something, but for now, your ass stays behind this glass."

"Aw, Cap, didn't know you cared enough for poetry," Chris replied jauntily. That humour again, she knew how worried he was about the kid.

Kara smirked, indulging him. "Get your butt in gear Anna, make sure he's comfortable in there and lock him up."

"Can I at least get a magazine…?" Chris grumbled as Anna walked him through, adjusting the bandages in case he ended up behind glass longer than they expected.

"Come on Chris, as if any of us brought the kinds of magazines you'd want." Anna poked at him playfully, "Big, tough guy reading Home & Garden."

"It's quality stuff!" He defended, "Tammy Lee has the best recipes!" Anna chuckled as she shut the door behind him.

"Divya, can you run through the last 6 days on the other cameras and still keep Dean on that screen?" She asked, motioning to the large projector screen.

"Yea, easy," Divya replied as she pulled up the feeds from the last six days on the computer in front of her. Kara stepped up behind her, she needed to know where the bodies had gotten to.

Chapter 5

June 10th, 2027 – Lab 3, 17:30

You're a complete idiot, Dean thought to himself, curled up as small as possible under the lab desk, making sure those things couldn't see him. He couldn't bring himself to call them people, not after seeing the dead glaze in their eyes and hearing the feral sounds they made as they attacked.

First real mission and you've thrown yourself on a live grenade. He replayed the moment he had made the decision in his head once again. Watching that thing tear a chunk off Chris and swallow it down like candy. Grabbing it from behind, then realizing his mistake as he broke into the Lab with it and hearing the others leap to life behind him. He saw the look in Chris's eyes again as he slammed the thing's hand onto the biometric scanner.

Well, at least I'm not cramped under here, he thought as he slowly stretched out one leg, feeling the pins and needles setting in as the adrenaline left his system. He listened carefully, straining to hear every movement the creatures around him made. What the hell were they? If they were zombies, like he had thought at first, he would expect them to be grunting, or groaning. That wasn't necessarily a fact though, he probably shouldn't be expecting this situation to be anything like the sci-fi books and movies he squandered his time on. Maybe they should be moaning and wailing? Or was that ghosts? He listened closely for a sound.

There it was, a chuffing noise. Almost as if they were trying to get something out of their throats, but couldn't quite make it. He heard it from one side of the room, then something, almost like a response, from the one closest to him.

There's no way these things are communicating, that was the last thing they needed, smart zombies. He heard the one nearest to him sigh, almost wistfully, as if frustrated at its inability to communicate. They seemed so helpless, he felt sorry for them, until he remembered the bared teeth, hooked claws and snarling as they raced towards him. He shut his eyes and thought back to the trip in on The Bus.

He was glad the Captain had decided Dante was his partner on this one. He liked Chris, but the man could be a handful at times. Dean remembered Dante clapping him on the shoulder as they left the loading dock this morning.

"Don't sweat it kid, we go in, we save some people, easy. You might even meet a pretty girl," the man had nodded towards Divya and winked at him. Dean chuckled, he didn't expect the guys to understand how he felt about Divya, but he couldn't stop them from joking about his nonexistent 'crush' on her.

"Not before me," Divya had smirked at them both, causing Dante to bark out a laugh at her forwardness. Dean had expected no less from the tiny Indian woman, she'd already told him exactly who she had her eyes on anyway. He'd checked his bag again and begun running through the plan once more in his head.

Dean let out a quiet breath and checked that his weapon was secure. He leaned back into the lab desk, his head coming to rest without a sound. The Captain had said she would get him out, and he trusted her. The only thing he could do was be ready when she made her move. The thing near him chuffed once more, starting up a new round of conversation in the room. Maybe he could learn a thing or two while he was in here.

§

"'The subjects showed increased levels of aggression in response to unexpected stimuli, most notably, any movement faster than their own speed,'" Divya read out to the team, "'with an immediate lack of response once the stimulus was removed from sight completely.'"

"So," Anna began, clamping her hand almost painfully onto Divya's shoulder.

Divya didn't complain as Anna continued, "basically they react until they lose sight of their target?"

"Basically," Divya responded as she scrolled through the documents she had found, reaching up to stroke Anna's hand reassuringly with her free hand.

"That explains what happened with Dean," the Captain mumbled as she read over her shoulder.

"Listen to this: 'No noted reactions to sound, other than general curiosity. No reaction to scent stimulus. Once exposed, there is no sense of self-preservation. Trials have been conducted. No survivors.'" Divya opened the file link on the screen before her.

"*Thrall stim test 11; Upon introduction of the element, there is no visible reaction to smoke and heat. No response to visual cues.*" They heard as they watched the animals on the screen before them burning, with no reaction. The flames in the room grew higher and higher. "*As with previous tests, once the subject has exceeded the capacity for pain of a normal, healthy subject, there is a response before termination."* The animals on the screen began to wail and screech, before abruptly going silent. Divya snapped the window shut, bile rising in her throat.

"Did he call them Thralls?" Kara asked, after a moment of silence.

"Well I guess they had to call them something," came Chris's muffled voice through the glass screen behind them. Anna had moved away, fidgeting with something by the lights. Divya knew the woman loved animals and hated that she had seen the clips.

"It's as good as anything," Kara responded, "at least we won't be calling them 'things' or 'creatures'. Divya, anything in there about how it's spread?"

Divya scrolled through the files, stopping to read when she needed to, "Yes Captain, 'Currently the virus is not communicable.

Subjects must be exposed directly to the gas, which disperses over the course of four hours.' I think Chris is safe." She continued searching for any updates on that information.

"Well there's some good news at least," Kara motioned for Anna to let Chris out of containment. Anna complied and checked his bandages once more before freeing him.

"Feels good to be out of the slammer," Chris said, stretching as if he'd been trapped in a small cell, as opposed to a large room. "So, 'Thralls' huh?" He asked, making his way to the computer she sat at. Divya nodded, continuing her examination of the files.

"Captain, there's nothing in here about how to change them back," Divya said quietly, the implications sinking into the team. Kara paused, weighing the decision before she made the call. She closed her eyes, briefly, and sighed before straightening her shoulders and looking around at her team.

"Alright, I'm authorizing the use of deadly force from here on out. We need to get Dean out of there. Any eyes on the bodies you saw before Divya?" Kara asked as she grabbed her weapon and made her way over to one of the cases they had brought in.

"Nothing Captain, the building is too dark," Divya flipped through the CCTV screens again, "There doesn't seem to be anything on this level though and from what I can see of the sub-basement, there's nothing there either."

"Alright, then we go down and get our man out." Kara dug three small, cylindrical objects out of the case and tossed one to Dante, one to Chris and kept the last for herself.

"Concussion grenades Cap?" Chris asked, turning his over in his hands, "You really know the way to a man's heart." He slipped the grenade onto the belt he wore.

"Flattery gets you nowhere Chris, and you're not going to be using that I hope." Kara pointed to Dante, "Dante, you and Anna are with me. Chris, you're on guard duty up here, we can't rely on those cameras right now."

"What's the plan Captain?" Dante asked as he stored the grenade and checked his weapon.

"We can't get Dean to open that door for us without endangering himself, so we lure them out. Last time it reacted to sound," she said as she checked the safety on her gun and patted her holster. Divya knew she was checking for her Ruger, "So we make some noise."

"You two stay safe. No one leaves this room until we're back," the Captain said, glaring at Chris and Divya in turn, making sure they understood the order. Divya nodded.

"Yes Ma'am" Chris saluted, clicking his heels together. She knew he understood the underlying order in her words.

They watched as the small team made their way out of the room and down the hall, checking shadows with their lights as they went. They had forgone the headlamps, not sure whether they would attract too much attention or not. Divya sat back at the computer, her attention shifting between the files before her and Dean, trapped in Lab 3.

§

Kara looked around at the two members of her team; she would have liked Chris in place of Anna, only because she hated the idea of their only trained medic being in the heart of fire. Unfortunately, with Chris's injury, he'd be more of a hindrance than a help at the moment. Anna was a fantastic marksman, she had no issues there, but if Anna was the one injured, there was no one on the team who knew any more than basic emergency triage to help. The lights in the elevator flickered as it descended.

"Do you think they know how to use these things?" Anna asked quietly.

"What?" Kara had been so focussed on her musings she had almost missed the question.

"Well, it's just that, the one that attacked Chris opened the door, right?" Anna sounded unsure of herself.

"If they do, they do, there's nothing more we can do but be prepared for it." Kara stated, sounding sure of herself. Anna straightened her shoulders and stood taller.

"Right," she affirmed as the doors to the dim basement hallway opened. They stepped out into the stale air, six days of no circulation did nothing for the feel of the room. It was stifling.

Kara's team swept the shadows with their tactical lights, painstakingly slowly, not wanting to trigger anything hiding in the shadows.

"All clear," she heard from Dante, followed by Anna and her own confirmation. She walked to the ComBox and radioed to Divya and Chris.

"We're all clear down here, how are you doing up there?"

"Just peachy Cap, spending a little quality time with my girl here," was Chris's response. The tension in his voice gave lie to his light tone though.

"Do you have movement?" She gripped the mic tighter.

"Not so much movement as shadows Cap," he responded seriously, "We can't see much on the other floors but something is out there." That almost sent a chill through her, almost.

"If you're done being ominous Chris," she chided, "We're going offline for a few minutes."

"What's—" She interrupted him before he could ask.

"It's basic, we set off the fireworks and see what comes out."

"Short and sweet, I like it." She could almost feel his grin through the speaker.

"Captain, should we fill Dean in on the plan?" Divya asked over the speaker. Kara had forgotten that she couldn't radio him. A small mistake but a stupid one, she couldn't afford to miss things like that, not today.

"Affirmative Divya, can you warn him over the P.A.? We don't want to spook him once they start moving." She paused to listen for the announcement and mentally berated herself for missing that detail.

No more mistakes from here on out Kara, she thought as she heard Chris's voice over the loudspeaker.

"Dean, if you can hear me I need a thumbs up buddy." There was a pause as Dean responded, "Good job, good job man. We got half the team outside that door right now, we're coming to get you. The Captain is using concussion grenades to draw them out, once they're out in the open it's a free for all, deadly force, so you stay the hell out of the way. If you get shot, I'm killing you myself, alright?" Another pause, and then a chuckle from the loudspeaker.

"I don't think the Captain would appreciate a rude gesture like that when she's coming in there just for you kid!" Kara shook her head at them and turned to Dante as Chris signed off.

"So, we just lob this down the hall and hope it attracts them?" He asked, tossing the grenade in his hand lightly. Kara nodded.

"That's the idea, nothing fancy. Get them out, clear them out and find Dean." She studied the hallway, "Our best bet is to make it around that corner of the stairwell before it goes off." They looked over to the darkest corner of the hall as she pointed. Dante nodded and shouldered his weapon, using the tactical light to guide his way. He reached the stairwell and slowly shone his light up the stairs, coming to rest on a white figure shuffling near the top of the stairwell.

"Captain," he whispered. Kara shouldered her own weapon and gestured to Anna to stay readied in the safety of the lights. She made her way to the stairs and her own light caught on two more figures, higher up. "How do we do this with them at our backs?" Dante spoke softly out of the corner of his mouth, afraid to catch their attention.

Kara had to think. If they took a shot at these three, they weren't sure what else they would bring down on them before they had the time to get Dean out. They couldn't see the whole upper stairwell either, so they had no idea how many thralls they were dealing with here. As she thought it through, she slowly swept her light across the stairwell, hoping to get a better view.

They couldn't move quickly, but the notes hadn't said anything about these things seeing in the dark, right?

Chapter 6

"Come in Command," Divya tried to reach Genotech once more on the external Com. The storm was wreaking havoc on communications and, as she had predicted, their handhelds were almost useless at this point, "I repeat, can you hear me?"

"It's no use kid," came Chris's gruff voice as he forwarded the footage she had accessed earlier, "Gotta wait 'til the storm's passed, then we get the hell out of here." Divya sighed and slouched in her seat. She felt drained already, and there hadn't been much physical activity on her part at all today. On the screen, she watched as one of the scientists sat down at a desk, probably checking their e-mail, doing something mundane, until disaster struck.

E-mail… she thought to herself. Straightening up once more, she rolled back over to the computer. *If I can just get an SOS out to Lindquist's Command Centre, maybe we can get some backup here.*

She tapped away at the keys with renewed determination as Chris walked over to the door check the locks once more.

"Got a plan?" He asked, peering out through the small bay of windows into the dimly lit hallway.

"Not so much, but if I can access their e-mail, I can send an SOS to Lindquist's team at Genotech. I just need to log in…" She trailed off as the screen flashed red before her. Two attempts later and she was greeted with the Genotech logo.

"Yes!" She hissed, "I've got it, I can access the Lab controls too, I can disable the locks if we need them."

"Well, what good will that do? We don't even know what's in that Bunker?" Chris quipped.

"Right, but once we do know, we can lock them in." Chris nodded at her statement.

That could come in handy, he thought and nodded silently as he watched her type.

"I can also do this," Divya said distractedly. Chris heard a beeping coming from the door and he turned to see the biometric panel shutting down. "Based on earlier, they obviously understand the mechanics behind biometrics, or at least, they retain the muscle memory of how to open these doors. Now we're the only ones who can get in or out." Chris grinned genuinely for what felt like the first time all day.

"That's my girl!" He exclaimed, clapping Divya on the back, "Always thinking, this one." Divya smiled tightly, still worrying about the rest of the team as she wrote out her e-mail.

"ERT, come in—Command. –epeat, come in ERT this is –mand" the external ComBox crackled to life as she typed. Divya stopped abruptly and dove for the receiver.

"Command, this is ERT, Lt. Kaur. We're getting some interference, can you read me?" She released the trigger and waited.

"—hear you Lt. Kaur. –access the main system. We can disengage the locks-- Bunker remotely." Divya froze for a split second before slamming the button down again.

"Do NOT! I repeat: DO NOT DISENGAGE THOSE LOCKS!" Divya shouted into the receiver. There was nothing but static on the other end. She turned frantically to Chris. Chris's tan skin was washed in grey as he turned to the screen showing their team. The doors to The Bunker and Lab 3 slid open as Chris dove for the ComBox.

§

Anna stood in the bright circle of their flood lamps. She held her weapon at the ready, waiting for a signal from Kara and Dante. She fidgeted with the strap of her M14, feeling constricted but knowing she had set it already. Nerves were a part of this job but she wished she could just ignore them sometimes. She had heard Kara and Dante speaking softly over at the stairs a short while ago, then their lights had gone dark. She wasn't sure what they were doing, but she had her orders and stood watch over the dark hallway. She adjusted her strap one final time before settling into her position once again.

Her mind travelled to Divya as she kept her eyes trained down the halls. She thought about small, reassuring touches, and smiles that she knew were only for her. The other woman wasn't as subtle as she thought she was. Anna smiled into the dim hall before she heard a small sound.

It was a soft hiss.

Almost mechanical.

She strained to listen and heard nothing else. Her eyes darted back and forth along the hallway. The entrance to the Bunker was around the corner, with Lab 3 further down that hall.

She knew this from their run in with those things, earlier.

Thralls… not 'things'…

She hoped Dean was okay in that lab. She heard muffled footsteps followed by a second hiss, and trained her light on the stairwell, looking for Kara, or Dante.

Nothing.

Maybe it was just my imagination, she thought, returning her light to the hallway before her as the ComBox crackled to life behind her, Chris's voice bleeding out of the speakers.

"Captain! They've disengaged the locks! Be ready to engage the enemy!" Anna, startled, aimed her weapon towards the Lab corridor as the first scientist shambled into view. She saw the Captain and Dante step out from the stairwell. At their motion, the scientist twitched towards them and dashed forward. Anna didn't give it a second thought, she took aim and squeezed the trigger. A rosette bloomed across the front of his lab coat but he didn't stop. Anna emptied three more rounds into his chest before he dropped to his knees and started crawling forward. Kara and Dante had taken aim, and between the two of them, managed to leave behind a mangled body as they walked forward and took aim at the other thralls rounding the corner.

It was over in seconds, clips emptied and bodies strewn across the floor of the corridor. They had fought their way to the lab doors, where Captain Piers called out to Dean.

"Dean, get your ass out here, we have a situation." She headed towards the elevator as they heard shuffling steps coming down the stairs. Dean stumbled out of the lab and followed them, weapon trained on the stairwell another thrall staggered out of the shadows.

§

Divya watched in horror as three thralls from the stairwell shambled into view of the camera. She had subverted a disaster by overriding the Bunker doors in time, but the thralls in Lab 3 had reacted to the opening doors, and made it outside before she could lock them in as well. She only barely stopped her hands from locking Dean inside the lab. She held her breath as the thralls dashed forward, almost inhuman. Her team, engaged in a silent battle, shot at them while waiting for the elevator to open. She felt Chris breathing down her neck as he watched one of the thrall's tackle Dante and drag his gun off him, even as it was riddled with holes. As the elevator doors opened, Dean grabbed the back of Dante's vest and pulled him through, shooting down a second thrall before it could reach them. The doors shut and Divya watched the remaining monster shut down almost instantly, milling around the corpses on the floor.

They're safe. She relaxed back into the chair and breathed a sigh of relief. She felt Chris relax minutely beside her as he reached over and flicked through the camera feed to find their hallway. It was still empty, but they kept the feed up as they watched the numbers of the elevator light up for each floor it passed. They kept watch until their teammates exited in a uniform line, watching each other's backs, with Dante in the middle. They didn't turn from the cameras until they could see their team through the bay of windows of Lab 4. Chris rushed to the door as Divya opened it to let them in. Dean and Anna kept their weapons trained until Dante and the Captain were safely inside. They holstered their weapons as they stepped into the secured lab and Divya locked the doors behind them.

"Well, at least now we know what we're up against," Dante huffed as he pressed an arm into his side.

"Here, let me have a look at that," Anna stepped forward and helped him to the small table at the back of the lab.

"Divya, what the hell happened down there?" Kara demanded as she approached the desk.

"I had to get into the Genotech system to e-mail out an SOS Captain," Divya started as she continued typing out her e-mail, "but I think I gave them back remote access to the whole building. They disengaged the lock on The Bunker, and I think Lab 3 opened with it. I can only assume they weren't getting complete sentences from me with this storm." Kara massaged her temples. Divya could practically *see* the tension in the set of her jaw and shoulders in her periphery.

"What about the Bunker?" Divya pulled up the feed she had managed to open and projected it on the bigger screen. Two shadows closest to the doors seemed interested in the noises from earlier, otherwise they could see a crowd of shadows milling about inside and dark stains on the Bunker floor. It was what they had suspected, the gas they had seen in the surveillance footage seemed to have affected the civilians in the Bunker.

"Can we lock the rest in?" Kara asked quietly, understanding that she was potentially condemning any survivors to death. If anyone could survive a week in that room, that was.

"I shut the doors as quick as I could, but yes. I can lock them if we need to," Divya replied softly and typed in a sequence. They watched as the biometric scanner in the room glowed briefly and turned from green to red. "Genotech will be able to override that with a little work, but hopefully they'll get our missive before they try."

"Dante? Anna?" Kara turned and headed beyond the glass.

"He's fine Captain, just a little bruising, nothing he can't bounce back from." Dante hissed as

Anna bandaged his ribs, "Oh hush, it doesn't hurt that bad." She smirked at Dante who glowered back at her in good humour, despite the situation.

"Alright team, new plan," Kara began rooting through the containers they had brought in with them, "We are assuming that there are survivors in that room, we're not about to leave them for dead." She pulled out extra clips for the M14's and passed them out.

"We also, apparently, can't depend on Genotech not to override Divya's program and open that door, so we'd be better off taking the offensive. Divya, any chance that the virus is still active in that room?" Divya turned back to the computer and opened the files on the virus.

"They mention here that it should dissipate within 4 hours, and once the ventilation system kicked in, it would have been fine." She opened another program; Kara could see pipes running throughout a diagram of the building. Some of the pipes were red.

"What's that?" Chris asked as he fit the extra rounds into his holsters. He'd had his specially made and it sat crossed on his chest. He said it made him look more badass when Divya had asked once.

"That's bad news is what it is," Divya muttered as she zoomed in on the red pipes. "The gas isn't fully vented, it's trapped in the system."

"Does that mean—" Anna covered her mouth, a gesture that would be too little too late at this stage of the operation. Divya found it endearing and answered in the negative.

"No, the effects of the gas are too immediate for it to be venting back into the building," Divya followed the red pipe until the image showed a ventilation filter with a red 'X' through it. "It looks like some of the filtration systems are offline and the water vapour didn't saturate the gas to diffuse it properly. The close quarters and humidity of the closed vents has also become the perfect environment to keep the gas in stasis."

"So, what does that mean for us Lieutenant," Kara asked. Divya stood up and walked over to the container. She reached into the bottom compartment and pulled out a large black case.

"It means," she said as she opened it up, "that it's a good thing Lindquist thought to pack these." She pulled out a gas mask and tossed it to Chris.

§

"So here we are, just like old times eh Dante?" Chris said jovially as he and Dante swept their tactical lights into the corners of the Lab 4 hallway. Kara had assigned them to clear out Lab 3 once they had figured out the situation with the pipes and they were headed to the elevator now. Chris adjusted the mask on his face, "Damn these are uncomfortable though."

Dante nodded in agreement as he pushed the button to the elevator and turned to sweep the hall once more with his light. He felt too calm, considering the situation they had found themselves in. Terrorists and acts of war were one thing; zombies were a whole other reality, one he never thought he would have to face. He jumped slightly as the elevator door dinged open and Chris looked at him curiously. Dante shook his head to let him know he was fine as they both stepped into the elevator.

You need to relax, he thought to himself as he rolled his neck and shoulders, *no telling what mistakes you'll make if you let this get to your head.*

Chris was still looking at him and Dante held his gaze for a few seconds. Chris seemed to find what he was searching for and looked away, adjusting the mask once more.

"We're getting out of this," he said, as he stared ahead, carefully keeping his eyes locked on the doors. "All of us."

Dante nodded once more. Chris always read his state of mind clearly, and usually knew what to say. He fiddled with the useless radio equipment on his belt. No matter what, he would be ready for whatever came next. He squared his shoulders and waited to reach the lower level.

§

"Divya, what's wrong?" Kara could practically see the furrowed brows and tense expression on her lieutenant's face, even if she was looking at her back. The screen in front of them had started loading a program a few moments ago, and Divya had been trying to cut into it before

Genotech did something else to affect the mission.

"This shouldn't be happening, I know they got that message, they had to have gotten it," Divya muttered in response as she continued trying to subvert the program. Kara walked over and placed her hand on Divya's shoulder.

"What's wrong?" She repeated, leaning over the other woman to read what was on the screen.

"Captain, someone is trying to vent the system." She stopped and looked at Kara. "If it vents, all of that trapped gas only has one place to go."

"The city." Kara said. "Can you stop it Divya?" She thought she knew the answer to that from the set of Divya's shoulders.

"No, I'm not familiar enough with the process to do it, and if I divert it, that will only send it back into the building, meaning…"

"Meaning any survivors or anyone not wearing a mask will be compromised…" Kara finished for her. "Help me pack a few of those extra masks. Once Anna and Dean get back, we need to get to the roof."

"Plan, Captain?" Divya asked as she rose to help.

"How long would you say that thing takes to load up?" Kara asked in response.

"The whole loading process takes about 45 minutes, probably an extra 15 minutes for them to vent the system, so we have an hour. Approximately."

"You said we might get the ComBox working if we were in open air, right?" Divya nodded, "Anna and I will take the shortest trip to the roof. We'll radio out to Lindquist and shut down the vent. You and Dean pack up and get ready for Dante and Chris to return. We regroup on the roof, it's as good a place as any for the remainder of this mission."

Divya had almost finished packing their bags when Anna and Dean returned. Kara filled them in quickly and they all set to work clearing the temporary camp they had created.

"Divya, I need you on that P.A. system, let Dante and Chris know what's going on. Anna, you ready?" Anna hefted her bag onto her shoulders, nodded and strode over to the doors. "Perfect, Divya, as soon as Chris and Dante get up here, I want all four of you out these doors."

Divya walked over and clasped arms with Kara. "You got it boss." Kara held her gaze for a moment before breaking the grip and heading towards Anna. Kara caught a glance between the two women as she walked past and looked away, giving them a moment of privacy.

"Let's go stop a tragedy Parsons," she said as Divya opened the doors to let them out. She heard her lieutenant's voice over the P.A. system as they made their way down the corridor towards the elevator.

Chapter 7

June 10th, 2027 – NCF Southwest Elevator, 18:45

"Dante, Chris, thumbs up if you can hear me."

Chris gave a start as the speakers above them crackled to life and spit out their names. He gave Divya two thumbs up and a smile for her trouble as they rode the elevator down to the sub-basement.

"There's a change in plans, Captain says to clear the lab, I'll lock it behind you. You just make your way back up here, pronto."

Dante and Chris exchanged a glance; there had been too many changes to this plan already, but they were nothing if not adaptable. Chris gave another thumbs up to the general direction he figured the camera was in. He made the motion of a question mark in the air as well, hoping Divya understood what he was asking.

"Genotech is trying to vent the system, Kara and Anna are on their way up to the roof, we're hoping they can get the ComBox working from there so we can stop them."

Damn it, what was the point of sending in a crack team of heroes if Genotech was just going to control the mission from behind a faulty radio connection and remote access anyway? He wasn't sure if Divya could see the expression on his face from behind the mask, but he realized she could when she continued.

"Yea, that's how we all feel right about now," she chuckled lightly and paused. She was gone for a few seconds before she came back on, sounding excited. "This message is for anyone who has not been infected. My name is Divya Kaur; I am with Genotech's Emergency Response Team. If you are in a safe position, please remain where you are. Once we have dealt with this current situation, we *will* be coming to help you. Please, *do not enter the ventilation system.* I cannot stress this enough, there are contaminants trapped in there and you will be exposed."

Chris grinned at Dante and offered his hand for a high five, which Dante graciously accepted. Why hadn't they thought about warning civilians in the building over the P.A. before? He listened as Divya continued.

"If you are in an unsafe position and can get close to the elevators located in the South West section of the building, please, get there and use those elevators to get to the first floor. We will remain at our base camp in Lab 4 for the next fifteen minutes." Chris stored that information away; they would have fifteen minutes to clear the lab and return to base.

"Please, avoid the stairwells, we have come across hostiles on them once already today. If you are trapped in The Bunker, make your way to the doors. Make sure you are moving as slowly as possible with no sudden movements.

Once I have the okay from my team, I will release the biometric scanner for a few minutes, please use it to exit and join my teammates." She paused once more and continued in a stern tone, "Remember to walk in a slow manner and do not make any sudden moves if you encounter a hostile. Do not take any unnecessary risks. If you are safe; Stay. Where. You. Are."

Dante waited to hear if she would continue. After a few moments of silence, he figured she was finished.

Just in time, he thought as the elevator came to a stop. He motioned to Dante to ready his weapon, but Dante was already ahead of him. They trained their weapons to the doors as they opened.

Kara ground her teeth as she listened to Divya's announcement across the P.A. system.

"Why didn't we do this earlier?" Anna asked, smiling up at Divya's voice.

"Not that warning them to stay put is a bad idea, but right now, it's probably one of the worst times to do it," Kara started as she and Anna slowly made their way up the stairwell. "At this point, if there are any civilians left, they'll be making their way towards that elevator."

Kara could see Anna's shadowy head nod so she continued, "And right now, we sort of need to *use* that elevator." Anna stopped.

"I didn't think about that." She could hear the grimace in Anna's voice.

"And I don't think that Divya really thought it through either, from the way it sounds." Kara knew her Lieutenant was only concerned about the safety of anyone trapped in the building, and so she could understand a rash decision in this situation. Unfortunately for them, even telling a scared civilian not to panic was an easy way to get them to panic.

"Let's just hope we can still do this the way we had planned on doing it," she muttered as they stepped onto the second-floor landing. "Dante and Chris should be in the sub-basement by now, so let's head over to the elevator and see what the situation is."

Anna stepped ahead of her and Kara turned around to cover her back. They walked in tandem, excruciatingly slowly, not wanting to bring anything down on them.

"Oh! Thank God, you're here! I didn't know what to do when I heard that announcement!" Someone shouted, running towards them. Kara grit her teeth and shouted back at the figure.

"Stop where you are!" The man, judging by the timbre of his voice, kept running across the office towards them.

"I'm a survivor!" He called out again.

"GET DOWN!" Kara yelled, training her weapon on the thrall who dove towards the man as he ran past it. The man screamed and dropped to the floor, thankfully, as moments later Anna and Kara opened fire on the attacking thrall.

Anna rocketed past her once they had it down and grabbed the man by the elbow. She dragged him up and spoke softly to him.

"It's okay, we're here to help." Kara elbowed her way between them and grabbed the man by his collar.

"What the hell were you thinking?!" She hissed into his face, "running out here like that?!"

The man whimpered slightly and had to swallow twice before he could answer.

"She said to head to the elevator if we could, I was holed up in one of the offices, but I made it out here and I saw your lights." Kara let him go and wiped her palm down her face. She knew Divya meant well, but this was just what she expected.

"She also told you to stay put if you were safe," she ground out, trying to keep her cool.

"Safe?! How could that even be considered *safe*?! Do you have any idea what's going on here?!" He was building up a good head of steam, Kara could tell, and she was in no mood to deal with it. Anna stepped in just in time.

"Sir. If you could come with us, we're heading towards the roof and—"

"The roof?!" He cut her off, "No. NO! She told us you had a camp set up in Lab 4 and that we should go there!"

Kara schooled her voice and spoke to him calmly. "She told you to meet her there in the next fifteen minutes. That was about five minutes ago, wasn't it?" He nodded. "And where do you think they'll be headed after they leave, in the next ten minutes?"

"To the roof." She knew he was just panicked. They were the first people he was seeing after dealing with this hell all week. She knew she should keep her cool and so she stepped back and allowed Anna to check him over. Her professional demeanor seemed to be just what he needed and he calmed down a bit.

"My name is Nick, Nick Wilson," he said quietly. Kara only nodded in acknowledgment.

"I'm Anna Parsons, that's our Captain, Kara Piers," she said as they took up their positions around him. "We need to head over to the elevator, so we're going to be moving nice and slow. Okay?" Nick nodded and they headed off.

§

"What the hell were they thinking?" Dean asked as Divya scrolled through the files on the screen. They were currently waiting for Dante and Chris to report back from Lab 3 so they could open the doors to the Bunker and catch up to Kara and Anna.

"I don't think we could understand their train of thought if we tried to Dean." Divya's expression had grown more somber with each file she opened. From what Dean could gather, the virus that had turned these people into Thralls was called the Black Virus, after its creator Caspian Black. Dean had heard about Caspian Black before; he was considered one of the brightest minds of BioFirm, Genotech's Biological Warfare Division. Not many people knew about

BioFirm, but Dean had run two missions in the past where he had dealt with their weapons. Those missions were exactly what put him on the Captain's radar if he was to really think about it.

Divya opened a video file on the big screen and they were shocked to see a man behind a glass wall, staring blankly out into the hallway beyond him.

"Oh god, don't tell me that's what I think it is?" Dean asked, feeling a mild trickle of horror seep down his back, cold and unnerving. Divya didn't answer, she just let the video play out. At first, the man just stood there, watching the figures on the other side of the wall. They weren't moving at all. As soon as one of the scientists started to make his way forward, the trapped man came to life. The two watched on in disgust as the man behind the glass tried to tear his way through the barrier to get to the people in front of him. The glass became marred with spots of blood and Dean had to turn away as one of the man's fingernails peeled clear off, causing his hand to leave wet, bloody trails after each failed attempt. When his hands wouldn't work, the Thrall began slamming into the glass, head first. Dean watched the blood pool and drip down the glass before he leaned over and shut the video off. He gave Divya a moment as he read through the files attached to the video.

"So, what it says here, about the virus being temporary?" He swallowed the bile rising in his throat at the idea that they had killed innocents. "Does that mean they'll turn back?"

Divya scrolled through the file she was reading.

"No, look here." She brought up the file on the big screen and highlighted a few sentences as she read them out. *"Currently, trials are being completed on large mammals with unexpected results... Within 6 hours, serotonin levels drop drastically, causing rage at unexpected stimuli. Levels stay low creating a rage cycle, leaving the brain without a way to raise its own serotonin levels.*

Permanent damage occurs." She pushed back from her chair and stood up angrily.

Large mammals, is that how they got away with this? Dean had had his fair share of run-ins with experimental weapons, and this whole situation reeked of it.

"So, basically, they tried to weaponize it, and those experiments were taking place down in that lab." Dean could feel the waves of irritation rolling off her. He walked over and placed a hand on her shoulder.

"Hey, look, everything is going to be alright." Divya turned into him and dropped her head onto his shoulder. He brought his other hand up and held onto her. They didn't have moments like this often, Divya didn't normally like physical contact with anyone but Anna. Since he'd started with the ERT he found she opened up to him easier when they were alone, and even then, only when she was distressed.

"It's not just the people here," Divya's voice was muffled, "I should have known there was something going on here. Kara expects me to be the intel of the mission and I feel like I led us in blind even before the lights cut. Now she and Anna are out there, everyone's split up. It's all on my back."

"Look at me." Dean pushed her back so he could look into her eyes, he could feel her tapping out a rhythm on his arm as he spoke, "There was no way of knowing what Genotech was up to out here, okay? No way at all." Divya didn't look convinced, and the tapping continued.

"Even if you had found all this information beforehand, don't you think there would have been a severe backlash from Lindquist and his hounds? And we would've had to go into this without you. Period." Divya's expression cleared a little and the tapping slowed, so he continued. "If you weren't here, we would never have known about those guys in Lab 3, we wouldn't have been able to shut those biometric panels and Kara wouldn't know to get to the roof. Right?"

Divya nodded as he made his points. He held her chin and looked into her eyes as he made his last point. "If you weren't here, there's no way we'd all make it out of this. But you are, and I know you'll get us out. How much longer do Chris and Dante have?"

Her change was almost immediate; a little pep talk was all it took for her mask to fall back into place. He'd gotten used to talking her out of these emotional pitfalls. Ever since he'd figured out her Anna secret, she'd been coming to him to talk about her crush at least once a week and he usually knew just what to say to raise her spirits. It came in handy in tense situations as well apparently.

Divya sat back down at the desk and pulled up the sub-basement cameras in time to see someone stumbling down the hallway towards Lab 3, with three thralls in pursuit. Divya was on the intercom in seconds.

"Chris! Dante! Genotech broke the locks on The Bunker! You've got incoming!"

§

Nothing.

A whole bunch of nothing.

No survivors, no information. Just bloodstains, a body and a lab that was in severe need of some TLC.

"You got anything over there Dante?" Chris called over to him.

"Nada, think we can head back to the ComBox and radio up to Divya?" Dante peeked around a bloody smear on the glass partition at the back of the room. He didn't want to know how that had gotten there. Before Chris could answer, they heard her on the P.A. system.

"Chris! Dante! Genotech broke the locks on The Bunker! You've got incoming!"

They heard the biometric scanner come to life and Chris made a lunge for the lab entrance as they heard someone shouting from the hall.

"Help! Don't shoot!" It sounded like a man, a kid really, the way his voice squeaked at the end of his plea. Chris hauled one of the scientists up to the scanner as Dante responded to the kid.

"GET IN HERE! I WON'T SHOOT YOU!" He had his weapon trained on the doors as the kid barreled in, followed closely by two thralls. "GET DOWN!" Dante shouted.

As the kid dropped to the floor, he opened fire on the thralls, who had slowed as soon as they lost interest in the kid. He had gunned one down when the kid decided to scramble backwards, out of instinct, drawing the attention of the remaining thrall and whatever was outside the doors.

"Chris! Get that thing closed!" Chris didn't waste time pressing the hand of his scientist onto the scanner, trying to shut the doors. Unfortunately for them, the first thrall had fallen right in the path of the doors. They snapped shut with a meaty thump and rebounded open again. An alarm began flashing in the Lab as a warning of an obstruction in the doorway blared overhead.

'*Please remain clear of the doors, as they are trying to close. Thank you for your co-operation. Please remain clear of the doors, as they are trying to close. Thank you for your co-operation.'*

Could this get any worse? Dante thought to himself as he moved towards the doors. With every repetition, that damn alarm was drawing more attention to them, and if The Bunker was open now, that meant there was a lot of attention to be drawn.

Out of his peripheral he could see the kid moving.

"What the hell do you think you're doing son!" He shouted over the rapid fire of his weapon. The kid didn't answer, he just stayed low and crawled forward. Dante could see the terror in his eyes as he made his way towards the very things he had hid from this whole week. The kid inched his arm forward and grabbed the coat of the thrall at the door.

Was he? He was.

He yanked as hard as he could, managing to clear the obstructed doorway as Chris slammed the hand back down onto the scanner. With a final hiss, the door shut them in.

"Nice moves kid," Chris huffed as he carefully set down the body he was holding up. "But in case you can't tell, you're a bit early to the party."

The kid looked haunted, was most likely in shock, but still managed to bark out a laugh. "I'd say you're the ones that are a little *late* to the party, don't you think?"

Chris laughed. "Chris Rodriguez, that there is my backup, Dante Alvarez. What can we call you kid?"

"Carr, Evan Carr." Evan pushed himself off the floor and offered his hand to Chris and Dante in turn.

"Well, Evan, we're here to rescue you. Though, at this point, I think we all may need rescuing."

Evan chuckled once more at that, "at least I'm not on my own anymore."

"Guess that answers my next question," Dante muttered as he checked the thralls left in the room for movement.

"There was one girl with me, she was just a kid," Evan started as he made his way over to one of the chairs and sat down. "She was there up until a few days ago. She didn't make her way to the doors though, so I don't think she made it." His voice sounded full, like he was talking through tears. Dante walked over and clapped him on the back.

"It's a hard place to be in kid. If she's still in there, we'll get her out. Don't worry." Evan sniffled lightly and wiped at his nose with a grimy hand.

"She had a gas mask on when I saw her last, I hope that keeps her safe when they vent the gas? That's what's going on, right? Why are you guys in such a hurry to get to the roof? I was listening to the lady on the P.A. earlier."

The gas! For a second there, Dante had almost forgotten the deadline they were on. Divya and Dean were waiting for them upstairs, and they now had no way to communicate with them, or a way of getting out of here.

Dante made his way to a small, black dome in the ceiling, where he assumed the camera was. He waved into it and mimed a phone. Divya's voice came over the P.A.

"Yea, this just got a whole lot harder. There are extra masks in your pack, you can give one to the guy. There's no way Dean and I can get through that hallway right now guys. I don't think we can even do it when the Captain comes back. You're going to have to go into the vents."

Dante sent her a quizzical look he hoped she could see.

"I sent all of the building's blueprints into our handhelds at the briefing remember? I sent backups of the files we found earlier as well. You can still access stored data from there if you need to, even if we can't communicate through them. There are vents and ladders leading to higher floors, find the ones that lead to the second floor and get your butts up here. I don't think this Lab will be safe for much longer."

Dante heard the change in her voice as she addressed any civilians in the building. "To anyone left in the building, the sub-basement is now unsafe, please remain where you are and do not try to wander the building as there are many more hostiles roaming about. My team will find you as soon as we contact Genotech for backup. Stay safe, we will help you."

§

"Dammit," Anna heard the Captain mutter under her breath as they listened to the situation downstairs unfold. It seemed as if Dante and Chris had found a survivor, but were now locked in Lab 3.

"Damnit all!" Kara muttered again.

"Does she always talk to herself like that?" Nick asked a little too loudly. It was as if this guy didn't understand how to whisper. Anna had found herself wondering how on earth he had managed to survive a week in this place as she learned more about him.

"Shh." She raised a finger to her lips to silence him as they crept forward slowly. After finding a crowd of thralls around the elevator on the third floor, they had made it up the stairs another two floors without attracting much attention. The only incident so far had been due to Nick stumbling up a step and drawing another thrall to them. Anna had dispatched it quickly, then Kara had turned on him and given him an earful. He had been sulking ever since, as if being chastised for his carelessness in this situation was something to be sulky about.

"If you're going to talk, at least speak softly." Anna could hear Kara grinding her teeth as she spoke to him. Kara was a stickler for gut instincts and had taken an instant dislike to this man. Anna couldn't blame her.

"I *was* speaking softly," Nick replied, too loudly once again. One of the thralls further up on the stairwell turned toward them and, with a low grunt, took one painstakingly slow step down. Anna stopped, holding onto the back of Nick's shirt to stop him as well. When he looked at her, she motioned to the thrall with her head to let him know there was danger around. Once the thing had lost interest, they continued up, coming across the fifth-floor landing and exiting out to the offices there.

"We can try the elevators on this level," Kara said as she shone her tactical light around the office. Soft light reflected from chrome surfaces and diffused off flat, dead computer screens. There didn't seem to be any movement on this floor. "If we can get into it, it will save us a lot of time."

"No way! Didn't you see how many of those, those *things* there were around the last elevator?!" Nick opposed as he backed towards the stairwell doors. "I bet there's even more *inside* the elevators! You said they could do that, right?" Anna grimaced at that, she had thought she was quiet enough when she asked Kara about that, but it seemed that Nick had heard her.

"Listen," Kara began, scrubbing her palm across her face. "There is an entire *city* full of people down there that need us to get to the roof of this building." Anna could hear the irritation building in her voice as the Captain hissed at him. "So, you have two options: Option 1 – You can come with us to the elevators, and we make our way to the roof of this building where we will save the city, shut the doors and be safe."

Nick stared at her defiantly, shoulders set stubbornly as he responded. "And what's Option 2?"

Kara turned on him and stared him down. "Option 2 is the one where I shut you into one of these offices, bar the doors and leave you behind until we *decide* to come back and get you. So, what's it going to be?"

Nick looked between the two women uncertainly. "You wouldn't really leave someone behind would you?" Kara didn't answer, she continued to stare him down. "Ms. Parsons, you wouldn't let her leave me behind would you??"

Anna kept her expression schooled and shrugged at him. "Nick, we need to get up there as quick as we can, now, I don't know about you, but I really don't feel like crawling up another 15 flights of stairs. Can we get to the elevator and get out of here?"

His shoulders sagged as he realized that no one was on his side. "Darcy will be hearing about this from me, I assure you," was all he said as he stepped away from the doors and gestured at them. "Well, go on. Lead the way."

Chapter 8

June 10th, 2027 – Somewhere in the NCF Building, 19:00

Riley crawled through the vents as quietly as she could. She had heard the announcements earlier, and she was kind of regretting leaving the Bunker now. Even if the team that had come were Genotech's lackeys, she'd much rather be with them than alone. That woman had sounded comforting anyway, maybe she could be trusted.

Stupid! If you had just stayed there you could be with people by now! She berated herself as she tried to find the right tunnel in this maze. She had crawled into the ventilation shaft a few days ago, hoping to find her way out of the building, or at least to an office where she could be safe.

She found she preferred the vents and had gotten to know them well in the last few days, managing to get to vending machines and lunchrooms to find food. Now, she needed to find help. She had listened to her aunt when she had told her to take a mask and keep it on, no matter what.

Tears stung at her eyes at the thought of her aunt. She hadn't made it out of that stupid room. Riley wished she could scrub the tears from her face, but the mask prevented that. She would just have to stop crying, that was all.

"Looks like it's time for us to make our exit!" She heard a voice echo through the shaft below her. If she could just meet up with them before they left, she would be safe.

Being with an adult was always safe, right?

She strained to hear anything else, anything that would give her a direction to follow and so she nearly jumped out of her skin when a loud *clang* echoed down the vent towards her. She knew there was a ladder in the shaft ahead. She made her way to it as quickly, and quietly as possible. She could barely make out a large number two sprayed on the wall near the ladder; she figured that meant she was on the second floor, so she needed to go down one more level.

I can do this.

She reached for the first rung and lowered herself into the black hole. She hadn't gotten used to the darkness yet since the emergency lights would leak into the vents before, lighting her way, but they had all shut off now. At least her eyes had adjusted enough to make her way around. She could feel her hands trembling as her imagination worked out the worst ways she could die and played them out for her viewing pleasure.

Finally, her foot touched down on solid metal. She could hear the weird grunting sounds those things made coming from a vent grate below her. She would need to be extra careful here. Her thumping had drawn their attention before, and even though they couldn't figure out how to get the vents open, Riley didn't really want those things trailing her for the next twenty minutes.

She stopped moving. Up ahead of her, she could hear someone making their way through the vents.

"You failed to mention how tight a squeeze this would be," she heard a man complaining quietly. The things beneath her shifted slightly, she could hear their sounds moving towards the voice. She wished he would just be quiet. If he drew enough attention, they could get aggressive, she had seen it before.

"I'm sorry for the inconvenience, at least you get a better view than I do."

The woman! The one from the announcements! Riley had to risk it. She crawled forward quietly. The things were following their voices anyway, they wouldn't be as interested in whatever tiny, little sounds she made. Up ahead, she could see a dim light making its way around a turn. She sped up slightly and called out to them quietly.

"Hello?" She heard a small collision from their direction. Then the sound of rustling cloth.

"Did you hear someone Div?" The boy asked softly. She heard something muttered and then the woman called out, just as quietly.

"Where are you?" The things below seemed to become agitated, if the increased volume of their grunts was any indicator.

"I'm coming up behind you, my name is Riley!" She would be safe! They were right there! They would get her out, and she could see her mom and dad again! She should have just listened when her brother had told her to drop the whole Genotech thing. Riley pushed forward and felt the grate give out beneath her. She caught herself on the lip of the vent and screeched as half of her body dropped out into the hallway.

No!

She was going to be safe now!

The things made a dash towards her swinging body and she screamed as she felt them grab her and drag her down.

§

Divya crawled through the ventilation shaft, listening for movement in the hallway beneath her. She could hear grunts from further ahead. Dean had led the way into the vents once they had made the decision to leave the base camp alone. She could see the mist curling in front of her headlamp as she crawled. She was glad Dean was trying to keep the mood light, it helped distract her from thoughts of Anna and Kara somewhere in the building, and Dante and Chris locked in the lab downstairs.

They won't be there much longer, she thought to herself. She knew that they would be heading into the vents as soon as they figured out their route. She traded banter with Dean as they made a turn in the vents. She heard something behind her and almost ran into the back of Dean, who had stopped.

"Did you hear something Div?" Dean asked her. She couldn't see him in the dark, but from his movements, he seemed to be trying to turn around in the tunnel.

"What is it, what did you hear?" She muttered to him as he came face to face with her.

"Sounded like a voice, couldn't be a thrall, right? They don't talk."

Divya curled in on herself to turn, and pressed into the side of the ventilation shaft, allowing Dean enough room to move past her. It really was a tight squeeze.

"Where are you?" She called out, listening to the grunts of the thralls below them become more agitated as they gathered together.

"I'm coming up behind you, my name is Riley!" Jesus, that sounded like a little girl. Divya froze as she heard her scuffling closer, frantically. Dean continued forward to meet the kid. She heard him shout as something metallic crashed into the hallway beneath them. She heard the thrall's grunts become aggressive as they dashed away from below her, and she felt Dean's disappearance from the ventilation shaft as a void of space in front of her.

Dean opened fire below her and she could hear the kid screaming. She needed to get down there. She made her way back to the intact grate and kicked it out. Flicking the switch on her light to increase the brightness, and swinging her headlamp out of the hole, she shouted out to Dean.

"Dean, I'm dropping in, when you see my light hit floor level, you two freeze!" She had already lost Chris and Dante; she couldn't lose Dean too.

"Keep your ass up there Divya! I've got the kid! You get to the roof, Kara needs you!" His voice was moving further away; he was probably backing down the hall. Divya didn't know what to do. She knew Dean could handle himself, but the kid. "Get out of here Kaur!"

It was the use of her last name that got her moving; he knew how to get her out of her head.

"Don't do anything stupid!" She shouted at him. She could hear the thickness of her voice as she whispered one last word, "Please."

§

Dean herded the kid before him as they rounded the corner. He heard the noises behind them stop as soon as they were out of sight and so he reined the kid in, trying to keep her from attracting any more attention. He could feel her laboured breaths as she crowded into his space, trying to make herself smaller it seemed.

"It's okay," his voice muffled through his mask as he tried to comfort her. He wasn't really that good with kids, there was usually someone else around him who could do better. "It's alright, they're not chasing us anymore."

The kid took a few deep breaths, amplified by the mask she wore. *Smart kid,* he thought as he tried to figure out their next move.

"I'm sorry," she whispered hoarsely. Dean realized she was near tears. "I'm so sorry. That was all my fault."

The last thing he needed was a hysterical child on his hands; he held her at arm's length, grasping her upper arms lightly. His mind flashed back to holding Divya like this just a few minutes ago, and he shook his head to clear the image before he became too worried.

"Listen kid," he started, looking into her eyes as well as he could in the dim light of the hallway. They hadn't even made it off the first floor and the lights they had set up earlier seeped into the hallway they were standing in. "This is not your fault. I need you to be strong for just a little while longer ok?"

The kid looked at him, he could see the light reflecting in her tearful eyes. She sniffled lightly and closed her eyes, her breathing evened out and the tenseness in her shoulders relaxed. When she looked at him again, the tears were gone and he could see something steely in her gaze.

"I can take this mask off down here right?" Was all she asked. He nodded to her and stepped back as she removed the mask and cleaned herself up a bit. He felt a little proud of her, being able to calm down like that wasn't something anyone in her situation could normally do.

"So, you got a name kid?" Dean asked as she replaced the mask and adjusted the straps. She looked at him, oddly calculating. He couldn't blame her for being cautious but still found it a little strange to see that look from someone who seemed so young.

"My name is Riley." She held out her hand, formally.

"Dean." He shook her hand. "You ready to get out of here then Riley?"

The change in her was instant, she grinned at him and gestured down the hallway. "Lead the way."

Chapter 9

"So, from what I read, these things are genetic experiments?" Chris talked as quietly as he could. Dante brought up the rear of their three-man train as they made their way through one of the larger vents. 'Larger' was an overstatement though, there was barely enough room for Dante's hulking figure, but Evan seemed able to walk comfortably. He was flanked by both soldiers allowing Chris to speak over his head to his partner.

"Biological Warfare. I've heard of Caspian Black before, haven't you?" Dante answered, they kept an eye open for anything in the vents, they didn't think the thralls would ever have a reason to be in here, but it was better to be safe than sorry. They had both read through the sparse files Divya had sent them earlier and were more cautious now that they had a better understanding of what they were dealing with.

"Yea, I remember something in the news a few years back. Didn't he help capture that insurgent camp without any casualties?"

"He's a genius." Evan interrupted, "he created the Black Virus to help solve conflicts peacefully."

"Peacefully?" Chris liked the kid, but he didn't need to see someone fanboying over an obvious failure and loss of life like this one.

"I don't know what happened here," Evan began, "Black Virus isn't supposed to do this. Caspian perfected it, it renders subjects docile and wears off after a few hours. This- This is something else."

"Subjects." Dante deadpanned. He wasn't too happy with the situation either.

"People, sorry. People." Evan corrected, sounding contrite, "I'm not used to real life applications. Really not appreciating the first-hand field test either, to be honest."

Correction, contrite and bitter.

"So, you seem to know a lot about Caspian Black, don't you kid?" Chris fished.

"I worked in the lab." Evan's voice was almost a whisper, "I—I tried to stop him, Jones, from opening the door but he shoved me aside and ran out." He was wringing his hands as he spoke, as if he was worried about what they would say.

Chris stopped and looked at Dante over the kid's head. Dante clapped the kid on the shoulder and squeezed lightly.

"You tried to save them." Evan looked up at them, surprised, as if he hadn't thought of it that way before.

"I—I did," he stammered again. Dante nodded to urge him to continue. "I was there, beside Jones' work station. I saw the gas leak before anyone else and managed to pull the alarm and grab a mask in time. Jones panicked. He had already inhaled the gas when he opened the specimen case. I could see how scared he was." Evan became choked up, reliving the nightmare.

"He knew it was over for him; we hadn't perfected it, or formulated a cure for this virus yet, and with the results we were getting from the live tests, it wasn't going to be a quick end for him." Evan inhaled deeply, leaned against the wall of the shaft and hung his head before he continued. "I practically saw the idea form in his head, but I couldn't do anything about it. He was closer to the door and I didn't make it in time to shut off the panel."

Chris and Dante stood around him in silence as he lowered himself to the floor and covered his face with trembling hands.

"All those people."

Chris knelt before him as Dante took up a lookout position.

"Hey, kid, look at me." Chris waited until Evan's soft, hitching sobs had calmed down a little and looked at him before continuing. "Listen. What you did? That was heroic alright?"

No wonder the kid had looked so haunted when they met him, he had been right at the heart of it.

"You didn't run. You didn't just look out for yourself. You tried your damnedest to keep those people safe, didn't you?" Evan sniffled and nodded. "And you did all of that, knowing *what you'd be trapping yourself in that room with,* right?" Evan's eyes widened.

"Oh god, I didn't even think about that!" Chris smiled reassuringly at Evan's horror-stricken expression.

"Well that just makes what you did even more heroic. And tell me something. What did you do in the Bunker? With that kid?" Evan paled slightly at the mention of the other kid.

"I tried to reach her, I was close to the doors, but I saw her moving around, she moved slowly, but different to the thralls you know?" Chris nodded, the kid was perceptive, and he had had enough sense to grab a mask when the drama started, no wonder he'd survived so long, "Well, anyway, I tried to find her but she kept hidden most of the time we were in there, I don't know if she even knew I was there. I should have talked to her but I was too scared of drawing attention to us." Evan was working himself up again and Chris couldn't have that.

"So, once again, you didn't think about your own safety, you were worried about someone else. You're a good man Evan." Evan looked up at him, wide eyed, registering the fact that Chris hadn't called him kid this time. "We're going to get out of this, okay?" Evan nodded and straightened himself up.

"You okay now?" Chris asked. Evan took a second, but nodded at him before he stood up and took his place between Chris and Dante once more. "Alright, now, you gotta tell us what you know about this virus."

§

"Thralls, that's what we had settled on calling them," Evan started. He was still feeling drained from his outburst earlier, but the big Latino guy had been surprisingly delicate with him. "Jones coined the term, he said that when the Virus took hold, it caused them to act as if they were enthralled by everything, moving so slowly and being distracted, etc."

The bigger man had led them to the first set of ladders and they were making their way up to the first floor from the sub-basement. The rungs were cold under his hands as he climbed, each step cleared his head a bit more. Evan continued once they had made it into the upper ventilation shaft.

"When Caspian had created Black Virus, Genotech saw the other implementations of the formula. I was part of the internship program here with BioFirm, Biological Warfare. You were right Dante." He heard a grunt from behind him and had to stop himself from reacting as if it were one of the thralls he had been trapped with.

"BioFirm wanted a weapon. Something they could drop in to permanently take out a colony of violent insurgents, or a terror threat, if they needed it."

"So, that's what this formula is then?" Chris interrupted him, "this is just BioFirm's latest weapon experiment gone wrong?"

Evan nodded. Then he thought about it for a second and responded.

"To be fair, it wasn't exactly a weapon gone wrong. The virus is doing exactly as intended. In the tests, once the virus is introduced into a host, it attacks the GABA levels in the brain and drastically spikes serotonin levels."

"English?" Chris asked, consulting his handheld and leading them down a right turn. They ended up in a long ventilation shaft that angled upwards.

"You sure this is right Chris?" Dante asked, sweeping the vent with his dimmed headlamp. Chris nodded and they started forward once more. Evan waited for more conversation, and when none came, he started talking softly once more.

"Serotonin levels are what keep you calm or enraged. Once the virus takes hold and those levels spike, the target becomes lethargic and unresponsive to stimuli."

Dante tapped him on the shoulder and shushed him when he turned to look at him. Evan got Chris's attention in a similar fashion and, when they stopped moving, he could hear grunting from below them. They moved forward in silence, until they couldn't hear it anymore.

"What's that on the floor up there?" Evan whispered to Chris as Chris shone his light down the vent.

"Looks like a hole in the floor." Chris sounded worried. Evan realized that it was probably because there was only one other team that would be in the vents. Unless this was caused by a thrall.

"Can we skirt it?" Dante asked. He sounded worried too. Evan hoped their friends were alright. Chris nodded in the dim light and motioned them forward. They could hear grunting from below and didn't speak to each other until they had made it past the hole in the floor and to the next ladder.

"So, I get that it calms them down, but why do those things attack? You're making it sound like Caspian had this all figured out, but that, down there," Dante gestured towards the floor beneath them, "that doesn't look like what you'd want on a controlled mission."

Even took a moment before replying.

"When Caspian perfected the formula, he took the qualities of dormant behavior and amplified it. He introduced a trigger into the virus, an enzyme that activated once attacked by the immune system and caused the virus to deteriorate. The Serotonin levels would stabilize and his targets would return to normal after a few days, as if they had just caught the flu or something." He tried to keep it as simple as he could, even though his better nature kept trying to get bogged down in details. "What BioFirm asked us to do was to create an offensive weapon; one that could permanently wipe out a threat."

Evan felt sick to the stomach, he had never really sat down and thought about the ethics behind the experiments. He had been accepted into Genotech's internship program and he'd been so overwhelmed at the idea of working with Caspian Black that everything else had taken a backseat.

"The current formula causes serotonin levels to rise, initially, which is what they wanted. The problem is that within 6 hours of exposure those levels drop drastically, and when they do, the targets experience rage at visual stimuli."

"So, do those 'serontonin' levels even out again? Why aren't these people going back to normal?" Chris asked.

"Se-ro-to-nin." Evan corrected before he answered. "Unfortunately, once the levels drop low enough, the targets become trapped in a rage cycle. Their bodies can't increase their own serotonin, and without the chemical, they cannot return to normal." Evan ran his fingers through his hair, this was a problem that had kept him up at night even before the outbreak.

"We've tried everything. Jones thought that introducing the chemical through an intravenous would help the system fight the virus, but there were no successful studies."

Chris nodded his head firmly, as if Evan had just confirmed something for him.

"Question," that was Dante behind him, "obviously the thralls retain some form of muscle memory, Divya showed us some of the camera footage, and we know that they can open doors, but do they have survival instincts?" Evan had overseen feeding the rats at the beginning of his internship and he could answer this one.

"It's a little strange, okay?" Dante just waited for him to continue. "Alright, so they do have some basic survival instinct. Something that is just predetermined in all of us I guess. Their bodies go into a sort of stasis, hibernation if you want to call it that?"

"That definitely ain't hibernating son," Chris supplied.

"No, *they're* not hibernating, but their bodies take on the qualities of it, the metabolism slows down, whatever small amounts of food or liquids they take in can last them for weeks." Evan remembered the white lab rats he had taken care of, he had been ordered to withhold food from them to see how long they would survive and the results had been disgusting, even to his scientific mind.

"Once their bodies start needing nutrients, they are not," he swallowed audibly, "they're not exactly picky about where the nutrients come from."

"You mean…" Dante sounded disgusted.

"Yea, they can survive on the dead for months."

Had he ever found these experiments acceptable? Had he ever really thought about them? How they would be applied to *people*? No. They were always just animals and reports on a computer screen. Now his life was one giant experiment gone wrong.

"Well, I guess we really are dealing with Zombies then huh Dante?" Chris, how could he already be joking about it?

"I hope Kara's on the roof," was Dante's response.

§

"So why are you guys here?" Riley whispered as Dean tried another white door in a sea of white doors.

Bet that one's locked too, she thought bitterly as she waited for his answer. Dean jiggled the handle and let out a gush of air, frustrated that every door they had come to had been locked tight.

"What? Did they calmly lock all the doors behind them as they left?" He muttered, shining his dimmed light down the hall, looking out for any wandering thralls.

"Actually, yea they did," Riley followed behind him as he started forward, "my aunt told me it's all part of the security protocols. If it's not a fire alarm, they get an announcement that tells them to lock all manual doors and make their way down to the Bunker."

Dean shook his head, clearly irritated at the fact that they hadn't been able to join the lady in the vents yet.

"What's her name?" Riley asked, part wanting to break the eerie silence of the halls, part general curiosity, "the lady on the announcements."

"Divya," Dean answered, trying another door, "and we're with Genotech. We're the Emergency Response Team under Darcy Lindquist, heard of him?"

Riley had definitely heard of Darcy Lindquist and when she had heard that the team that had been sent in was involved with him, she had become immediately distrustful of them. She needed to get out of here though, so she would need their help.

"I've heard of him before, from my aunt. She would keep her answers vague then, "She didn't tell me much though. Most of it was while we were in the Bunker. Before they started turning. Once we knew it was real, she said they would be sending a team because of the leak, I guess that's you?"

Dean nodded, "At your service."

Riley didn't want to like him, but this guy was friendly, and obviously very brave. She thought back on how he dove out of the vents behind her when she fell. A guy like that couldn't be all that bad, could he? Maybe he didn't know what Lindquist did? All the lives he was responsible for taking? She could probably find out with a few more questions, but she didn't want to draw his suspicion.

"So, did you work here?" It seemed that she didn't need to push him to talk at least.

"No, I was just visiting my aunt for the day, I do that sometimes when mom and dad are busy," She could be honest about that much, she had left the camera behind when she escaped the Bunker, but she didn't have much evidence on there anyway. "Picked a hell of a day to visit, didn't I?"

Dean snorted lightly at that. She decided to push for a little more information; if he was asking questions so could she, right?

"How did you get stuck with *this* job?" She asked. Dean tried another door before answering.

"We're actually the only ones at the base right now. The others are on another mission. So, just lucky I guess?" He turned and gave her a crooked smile. "You think you're ready to brave the vents again?" He asked as he swung the door open. Riley grinned and stepped into the room behind him.

"Hell yeah!" She replied with as much force as she could in a whisper. Dean chuckled once more and swept his light around the room. There was a body on a chair in the corner. It was facing the wall, and Riley stopped herself from gasping before pressing her back against the wall and slipping a hand between the door to keep it open. Dean inched forward, not wanting to draw the attention of the thrall. When he reached the body, she saw him relax, so she called out to him softly.

"Dean, is it ok?" He took a moment before answering.

"Yea, it's ok. Just give me a second to clean this up."

Clean it up? Clean what up? Riley didn't give him a chance, she allowed the door to shut with a *snick* and strode towards him.

"What is it?" She asked as she rounded in on the body. For the first time in a long time, she wished she had just listened to an adult. It was a man, she thought it was a man by the bloated shape beneath the lab coat at least. He was missing the top half of his head, Riley could see chunks of black and grey matter dotting the back of the chair he sat in, and there was a dark stain flowing down the back and shoulders of his coat. She turned her eyes away from the sight before her and noticed the small pistol on the floor beneath him.

"I told you to let me clean it up," Dean said softly, placing an arm around her shoulders and leading her away from the mess. She was grateful as she had closed her eyes and was trying her hardest to clear the image from her mind. Flecks of grey matter dotted the darkness behind her eyes and she screwed her fists into them to stop it.

"Hey, Riley, breathe," she heard Dean's voice and latched on to it. She opened her eyes and realized she had gone weak at the knees and was now on the floor. "You gonna be okay?" Riley gave herself a few seconds to school her voice before answering.

"I'm fine." She took a deep breath and lifted herself off the floor, taking Dean's offered hand to do it. She wasn't going to deny his small act of comfort, and she would be lying if she said the contact didn't help to calm her down further. "I just needed a minute there. Do you think he's been like *that,* for long?"

Dean stayed at her side and looked back over at the corpse.

A real corpse, she thought, *not like you haven't seen enough of those this week.* Although, corpses didn't have a habit of getting back up and walking around, she had to admit.

"By the looks of it, he's probably been like that since the beginning of this whole thing? Maybe 5 days?" She saw him grimace and wondered what that was about. He answered her almost as soon as she thought it though.

"Look, do you know how to use a gun?" She looked at him blankly before registering where he would get the weapon. She cringed visibly.

"OH, ew, I'm not using that thing!" She backed away from him with her hands held up, as if fending the thought off. "Besides, no I don't know how to use a gun." She had been meaning to get her dad to teach her, but had never gotten around to asking him.

"I can give you a quick lesson. I've got my handgun, but judging by the looks of you, it would be way too big for you to hold, let alone use effectively. That thing though?" He gestured at the weapon lying on the floor, "it looks like it would be just the right size for your tiny, little, baby hands." Riley watched him smirk as he said that last bit and she glared at him, knowing he was doing it to rile her up.

"Tiny. Little. Baby hands?" She ground out, causing his smirk to grow into a full-blown grin as she played along.

"Yea, so you need a tiny, little, baby pistol. Sound good?" He looked at her hopefully, the ghost of his grin still playing on his face. Riley tried to stifle the thoughts of *'dead man's gun'* and *'that's so gross'* as she nodded. She watched as Dean walked over and picked up the pistol. She turned away as he cleaned it off.

"You're in luck, nothing on it." She heard him rifling through the drawers, "and it looks like he's got ammo, which is great because you're probably a terrible shot so you'll need as much as possible." Riley heard the smile in his voice as she turned around, looking mock offended.

"Excuse me, I bet I'm a fantastic shot!" She could play this part. She had missed the back and forth between her brother and herself this week, something she would never admit to his face, of course.

Dean's jokes were comforting.

Dean chuckled and returned. The small pistol was unassuming and didn't look deadly at all. Riley glanced back at the man in the chair and gulped as she took the gun from him.

He showed her how to hold the pistol properly, making sure she knew enough that no part of her would get caught in the mechanisms. He showed her how to reload, and she watched intently, being sure to get it right. When he was confident that she knew enough to get by, he led her over to the vent.

"We're going to need to push the desk over so we can get up there" he said, walking back over to one side of the desk, and gesturing to the other for her to take her place. She walked over and helped him drag the desk over. In all honesty, Dean did all the work, Riley was preoccupied by a thought that had entered her mind as she struggled to push her end of the desk.

"Hey, Dean?" She asked, walking on the spot as the desk fought back against her. Dean watched her for a second before rolling his eyes and helping her push her side up against the wall.

"What is it?" he huffed out, pushing his dark hair back from his forehead before hopping up onto the desk and offering her a hand.

"I was just thinking about it." She grasped his hand and hoisted herself up. She felt her bare hand slipping from his gloved one for a split second before he tightened his grip and hauled her up. She gave herself a few heartbeats to calm down and continued. "Why does that guy even have a gun? Or ammo? I mean, what kind of a person keeps a gun in their office drawer?"

Dean was silent. Riley couldn't read the expression on his face since he was facing the wall, trying to pry the vent off, so she couldn't even guess at what he was thinking.

"I dunno kid, maybe he just liked showing it off?" The use of the past tense didn't slip past her, she swallowed her emotions at the thought of how many 'past tense' people there were in this building. The grate came off the wall with a low screech.

Genotech… she thought angrily as she fastened the mask to her face and allowed Dean to boost her up into the ventilation shaft, turning around to help him one she was secure. This vent was big enough for both of them to crawl along comfortably in. When the shaft widened enough for Dean to stand, he pulled out a small, handheld device. The light from it lit up the shaft in a dim glow.

"We're in luck," he said, turning as much as he could to grin at her. "The ladder up is just ahead, and it goes up a few floors." His grin was contagious.

"So, we can catch up to your friend?" Riley asked, glad for the news of more people; a bigger group might mean better odds of survival.

"Yep," he checked his map again and put it back, before heading further into the shaft. "Come on, this way."

BLACK VIRUS OUTBREAK

Chapter 10

June 10th, 2027 – NCF Heading to the 20th Floor, 19:25

Kara had had enough of this insipid man. They had finally made it into the elevator and had begun their journey up, and all he had done was complain.

At least now we don't need to keep shushing him. That was getting annoying fast. Nick spoke up as she thought this.

"You do know that I'm a close, personal, friend of Darcy, right? You might call him Mr. Lindquist," he said condescendingly to Anna. Once he had realized that she wasn't on his side, he had quickly had a change in attitude towards her. "I just want to let you know, because you should treat me how you would treat him." Poor Anna was cornered as he spoke to her, but Kara couldn't help. If she tried, she was likely to end up knocking the man out.

She didn't normally have anger issues like this, but the absolute mess of a mission and this man's blatant disregard for their safety had her on edge. Not only was he endangering himself, he was also endangering her partner. With every noise he made, he drew the attention of thralls near them. At one point, she had actually needed to clamp her hand over his mouth when he had stepped, ankle deep, into a soft, bloated body and almost shrieked, right in the middle of a pack of the things.

I guess pack is as good a term as any? Like a pack of wolves? She thought, trying to distract herself from his incessant chatter, while keeping her weapon trained on the door, in case they were stopped on the way up. Nothing of the sort happened. Kara watched the numbers light up as they made their way up. She wondered what the rest of the team was doing, and hoped that Chris and Dante had made it to the first floor before Divya and the kid left.

"Kara," Anna's voice broke into her thoughts. The pretty brunette had sidled up to her in the elevator, "we're almost to the top floor." She indicated to the numbers Kara had been staring at and Kara refocused her attention on them, only to see that Anna was right. They were almost at the 20th floor.

"Top floor? I thought we were going to the roof!" Kara didn't bother answering, and so the task fell to poor Anna.

She's getting extra vacation days after this, her and Divya both, Kara thought, shooting a small smile at Anna.

"We can't get to the roof from the elevator Nick," Anna explained, as if talking to a toddler Kara mused.

He might as well be, Kara needed to stop this, she couldn't keep this animosity towards Nick up; it was distracting her and keeping her on edge. She took a deep breath and pushed her irritation down. She turned and looked at Nick, her voice taking on the same gentle tone Anna had been using this whole time.

"We just have one floor to get through, Mr. Wilson." She hoped the calm and respectful tone she was using would help him to relax. "It's a straight shot to the roof exit once we get out of here."

"And then we lock the doors behind us?" He sounded cautious, as if he didn't trust this new Kara. She didn't blame him. She wasn't even sure how long she could keep this up, thank god she had Anna to back her up when she needed to step away.

"Yes Nick," Anna stepped up. Kara moved to the doors and pressed the door close button.

They were on the 20th floor.

"We don't need to leave the doors open behind us, the rest of the team are on their way up through the vents." Anna finished, checking her weapon as she spoke. Making sure they were prepared before they left the safety of the elevator.

"Well, why can't we use the vents?" Nick asked, sounding as if he was offended by not being offered that option. Kara bit back her answer and allowed Anna to handle it.

"Nick, we're only one floor away from the roof, it would take more time to find and use the vents than it would to just walk to the other side of the offices."

Nick seemed as if he was contemplating the idea and Kara kept her finger on the elevator's close button, not wanting to be talking out on the floor. She waited for what felt like a lifetime while he made his decision.

"We could always leave you in here?" She couldn't help it, but she wasn't really saying it to be malicious, just to get a decision out of him. "You can close the doors behind us and keep them closed until we come back?"

"That's not even an option!" He sputtered out, the edges of terror creeping into his voice, "it's bad enough that you people had me leave that office, now you just want to leave me out in the open, undefended like this?!"

Kara held herself back from pointing out that it had been his decision entirely to leave the office, when Divya had told them to stay put if they were somewhere safe. She waited again, finger on the button, as he came to his slow decision.

"Fine, let's go," Nick straightened up and stepped behind Anna, as if using her as a shield. Kara was actually annoyed at this, even though that was generally their job. Kara adjusted the portable ComBox on her shoulder and readied her weapon. She looked to Anna, who nodded to her, signaling her readiness. Kara took her finger off the button, stepped into the darkness of the office beyond the elevator, and swept the shadows slowly with her dimmed tactical light.

"Shh!"

"What is it?"

"I think I see something up ahead"

"Ouch, watch where you're going kid."

Dean shook his head and smiled at the sound of Chris's voice. He turned his headlamp back on and shone it down the vent at the other team.

"If you three make any more noise you'll wake the dead," he said, grinning and releasing his hold on Riley, who had aimed her gun at the first sounds coming down the shaft.

"Well aren't you a sight for sore eyes!" Chris exclaimed as they drew nearer. He reached out and clasped Dean's hand roughly with his mangled paw, "and," he paused as he turned to the small figure beside them, "you're not

Divya…" he concluded, looking beyond Riley's small frame for the slim woman. Dean sighed.

"We got separated and I found this one about to be something's dinner." He saw Riley visibly wince. He hadn't meant it in a mean way, he'd never expected a kid to take such good care of themselves and yet here she was, one of the only two survivors they had found so far. He was proud of how she had handled herself.

"Well, and who would you be little bit?" Chris asked, flashing a charming grin at the little girl. Dean could hear the strain on his voice though, he knew Chris would be worried about Divya; she was pretty much his favorite person, second to Kara.

"My name is Riley—" She didn't even get a chance to finish before the young man with them interrupted her.

"It's you!" He exclaimed, squeezing past Chris's hulking frame and approaching the girl. "You're the girl from the Bunker!!"

Riley stepped back in the face of his enthusiasm and looked at him quizzically.

"How did you know I was in the Bunker?" She asked, seeming shy suddenly. Dean couldn't blame the kid; she was stuffed in a vent with four large men.

Well, three large men and a lanky boy at least, he corrected himself and hid a smile.

"I was in there too!" He didn't get any closer, Dean was glad the guy could tell she was uncomfortable, "I didn't see you for a few days and I was worried you didn't make it." Dean couldn't tell in the dim light, but he was sure the guy was blushing now. He could practically hear it in his voice. The guy turned to Chris and grinned at him. Gesturing towards Riley he said, "She made it!"

"Yea, she did Evan." Chris's tone was gentle, like his smile. "Told you she would." Dean wondered at that conversation, Chris Rodriguez wasn't always the gentlest of guys; Dean had the bruises to prove it.

Guess he has a soft spot for kids, he thought as Chris clapped him on the back, *and speaking of bruises*, Dean winced as Chris steered him away from Evan and Riley. Dean looked back and received a nod from Riley; she seemed to realize that he was concerned about her. He flashed her a smile and allowed Chris to lead him over to Dante.

"So, you got separated?" Chris cut straight to the chase. All traces of gentleness from earlier gone, he was all business now.

"Yea, the kid fell out of the vents trying to reach us, I ended up on the ground with her and I told Div to get to Kara," Dean summarized. "It happened about twenty minutes back, and we had to find our way back in here so Divya should be close to rendezvousing with Anna and the Captain." Dante's face was tense as the two men absorbed the information he laid out.

"Alright, let's get these kids moving, we have places to be and not a whole lot of time to get there." Chris turned and walked over to the two survivors: "You two about done catching up?" Dean wasn't sure, but he'd bet that the lanky guy was blushing again. His mind wandered to Divya, he hoped she had made it to the rooftop and was safe with Kara and Anna.

§

Kara saw it happening before she could stop it. Anna had taken up her position in front of Nick, with Kara bringing up the rear. Nick had been muttering non-stop under his breath and Kara hadn't said anything. He wasn't loud enough to attract attention and she didn't have any more patience left to talk to him gently.

"There's something up ahead," Anna whispered back to her, leading her light to a thrall further up. Kara tensed as she watched the thrall flinch away from the dim light and turn in their direction. The thing was twitching and moving around as if it was in pain. She brought her weapon up as it took a step in their direction.

"It's just another one of those things," Nick whispered harshly. At least he was keeping his voice down. "The roof exit is up there right?" Kara reached out to stop him as he muscled past Anna and took a step towards the thrall. Her fingers only brushed the rough material of his jacket as he stepped out of her reach.

Anna reacted faster than Kara could. The thrall came to life as soon as Nick stepped close. It screeched as it lunged blindly at him, fingers becoming ragged claws. Kara shone her light into its eyes, hoping its reaction before wasn't just a poorly timed twitch, and was rewarded for her gamble as the thing screeched again, clawing at its blind eyes.

Kara had caught a glimpse of raw, red and bloody sockets in place of its eyes and wondered how it had known where Nick was in the first place. The thought was thrown to the back of her mind as she watched Anna step forward and push Nick behind her. The ridiculous man stumbled backwards, shouting and knocking Kara's weapon out of her grasp. Kara fumbled for her gun as her tactical light caught on other figures crashing through the desks around them, drawn by the commotion they were creating.

"Coming in from the sides Anna!" Kara called out, getting her weapon under control and pointing it at the nearest thrall, taking him out at the knees.

Nick, panicked and shouting, stumbling towards the roof exit. He pushed Anna to the side, into the claws of the blind thrall.

"What the hell are you doing?!" Kara shouted after the man, who turned to see what was happening just in time. Anna screamed and dropped to her knees as the thing clawed into her face, tearing three ragged strips down her cheek and almost taking out her right eye.

Kara was at her side in moments, training her weapon on the thrall and tearing into its stomach with a rain of bullets. "I have you Anna, can you get up?" Anna nodded, pressed her gloved hand to her cheek and straightened up. She turned and took aim at the other approaching thralls with her free hand.

"Get to the doors Kara," the woman commanded, firing into the oncoming mob. "We need a clear way out of here. Grab Nick and get up there." Kara turned and made a grab for Nick, who had fallen on his backside and scrambled back to the base of the staircase when Anna had been attacked.

"Get up!" She hauled him to his feet and dragged him up the stairwell, shooting at anything in their path. She could hear Anna behind her, firing bursts at anything that moved and using the occasional single shot to clean up after Kara. Kara had released Nick and he was stumbling along between them, mumbling as he ran.

"I'm sorry, I'm so sorry," he gasped out. Kara didn't know if he was apologizing to her or Anna, but it didn't matter, apologies weren't helping them right now.

"Just shut up!" She shouted at him, she didn't need to keep her voice quiet anymore, the mob behind them wasn't losing interest any time soon. There were no barricades or corridors to turn down to get out of sight and, as she looked back, she could see the ones Anna hadn't managed to finish off crawling up the stairs after the rest.

"Kara! The door!" Anna took out another thrall that came too close for comfort. Kara reached the metal door and wrenched her hand back as static arched towards her outstretched limb.

"What the hell was that?!" Nick shouted into her ear, cowering between the two women.

"Anna! I need your glove!" She took aim as Anna divested the glove and tossed it back to her.

"We're not gonna make it! There are too many of them!" Nick was blubbering now, grasping onto the back of Kara's vest and practically dragging her down with him.

"Stop that!" Kara shoved him off roughly as she pulled on the rubberized glove and wrenched the handle down. She pushed against the door but it wouldn't budge.

"There's a keypad!" At least Nick was being helpful amidst his hysteria. "There's a code to open it but I don't know what it is, I've never needed to get out there. We're trapped!"

Code, code, I remember Divya telling me something about the code. Kara wracked her brain for it, she worked best under stress and took a moment to calm her mind. It came to her easily.

"Kara, the roof exit is electronic, it's one of the four that Lindquist said are continuously powered. The general maintenance code is 7273." Divya had been handing her the portable ComBox. *"When you two get to the roof, you'll need this to contact Lindquist."*

"Got it!" Kara reached over and keyed in the code. Nothing.

"Anna, it's not opening." Kara wasn't sure if Anna had heard her horrified whisper over the intermittent bursts of fire. Kara slammed her gloved fist on the locked door, "it's not opening goddammit!"

"Grab Nick!" Anna reached back between shots and shoved the man further up the stairs towards Kara. "Shut your lights off Kara."

"Anna, no." Kara reached for her medic and shot over her shoulder at a thrall whose mouth had been torn into a horrible grin of fully exposed teeth. There was a spray of flesh and bone as his grin bloomed into a black hole, "You aren't doing this." Kara felt Anna's hand tighten around her own for a moment. She felt as Anna drew back and shoved her backwards.

"Anna!" Kara grabbed for her arm, or whatever she could reach, and missed. Anna shouted to the man behind her as Kara stumbled backwards, up the stairs.

"Grab her!" Kara felt Nick's arms encircle her torso and struggled against him.

"Parsons you *do not* have my permission to do this!" Kara put as much force into the command as she could, hoping to stop the woman from making a huge mistake. "Get back here!"

Anna turned, and in the moment before the thralls reached her, saluted. Then she was turning and firing at them once more.

"Anna! Catch!" Kara wrenched her M14 over her head and threw it down to her medic, pulling her Ruger from the thigh holster she kept it in. Kara maneuvered so that she stood behind Nick, hand clamped firmly over his mouth, weapon trained down the stairwell. There was no way she was going to let Anna sacrifice herself in vain. They sat in complete darkness, Kara could feel Nick's deep breathing as he sagged against her. She was certain he had fainted.

She watched Anna shoulder her way through hands that clawed at, and slipped off, of her body armor. Anna reached the bottom of the stairs and Kara watched as the thralls surrounded her. Kara refused to turn her head.

She saw the lights blocked out and listened as the random bursts of gunfire slowed. Kara heard a heart wrenching scream and the gunshots disappeared altogether.

Anna, Kara waited a few moments as things quietened down. There didn't seem to be any of those blind thralls with this crowd, thankfully. If there had been, then Anna's choice would have been worthless. She felt Nick struggle against her hand and whispered to him.

"If you make so much as a peep, I *will* throw you down there for them." Kara felt his nod and released her grip on his face. Nick stepped away slowly and Kara could hear sniffling. She had bitter thoughts at the idea of this man shedding tears for Anna but kept them to herself. She was grateful for the moment Nick gave her before talking though. She never expected him to keep silent for long.

"I guess we're using the vents after all?" Kara hung her head, she couldn't believe the smug tone she heard in his voice. Come to think of it, she wasn't surprised at all. "Well, lead the way then?"

"We wait here for a few minutes, let them disperse." Kara sat on the top step, fingers tracing her gloved hand. "Then we go down to the offices."

She felt Nick sit down beside her and turned away from his shadowy form. She could hear tapping on the metal behind them and slapped at Nick.

"Stop it, you're going to attract their attention," she growled, grabbing his hand to silence the sound.

"That's not me," Nick wrenched his hand back from her grip and stood up. "It's coming from the other side of the door."

Oh god, don't tell me they're outside too. Kara stood up slowly and turned to face the door. She placed her gloved hand on the door and felt vibrations. She felt the door shudder and heard

the screech of metal on metal. Kara backed down the stairs, holding her Ruger ready, waiting to see what came through. She felt Nick grab onto her vest again and shrugged him off. She needed unhindered movement to deal with this.

Two more bangs and the door shuddered one final time.

Those things are going to be making their way back up here now, I'm so sorry Anna. They were surrounded. Light peeked through the edges of the door and Kara levelled her weapon at the oncoming threat.

"Kara, is that you?"

Divya! Kara was dumbstruck, she hadn't expected to hear that voice at all; they must have left the Lab earlier than they planned. Nick pushed past her and shoved the door open. Kara heard Divya grunt in pain as the door caught her and she grit her teeth.

"We're here!" Nick shouted, pushing through the door to the roof, with Kara on his heels. Kara turned and slammed the door shut again, catching a glimpse of the thralls at the bottom of the stairwell and a bloody M14 discarded at their feet.

"Kara, where's Anna?" Divya sat on the gravel of the rooftop, knocked down by Nick's exuberant dash through the door. Kara looked at her Lieutenant with blank eyes. She couldn't even bring herself to tell Divya what happened. She almost didn't need to. She watched the light dim in Divya's eyes.

"No, no she's not." Divya wrapped her arms around her knees; Kara could see the tears welling up behind her mask. "Kara, please tell me she's not." Kara walked over and dropped to her knees beside the young woman.

"I'm sorry Div, I know how important she was to you." Kara wrapped her arms around her and pulled her in, "I'm so, so sorry." Divya broke

into tears, ripping off the mask and tossing it down beside them. Kara held her as the sobs wracked her body, and she felt her own tears begin to trace their way down her cheeks.

Anna hadn't only been important to Divya. Kara had personally requested her to join their team after seeing her in action on a mission with the German sanction. Kara had been called in to help with an evacuation and had been impressed with the medic's cool head and calm attitude.

It was no surprise the woman had done what she had done.

Kara smoothed Divya's hair down, it was sticking up in places after being treated to a gas mask and the errant static in the air. She looked around for Nick and saw him brooding at the edge of the rooftop. A glance to her side showed her some wires leading from an electrical box to the door they had come through.

Trust Divya to figure out a way to ground a door with a pair of tactical gloves and some wire, she smiled softly at the woman in her arms. Her sobs were starting to taper off and Kara needed to get that message out to Genotech. Before she could say anything, Nick stepped away from the edge of the roof.

"Could we just get on with this," he started, sounding more annoyed than he had the right to be, "I know what happened to your friend was bad, but we should get out of here as soon as we can." Kara felt Divya stiffen in her arms. She glared at Nick as the younger woman's sniffles slowed, and stopped. She hated that he was right, they did need to get a move on. Divya stood up, bringing Kara with her, and stepped out of Kara's arms.

"Do you have the ComBox Kara?" She asked, her eyes were bloodshot and her dark skin was flushed, "Let's get out of here."

Chapter 11

June 10th, 2027 - Off the NCF Compound, 19:25

"How is the venting procedure coming along?" Devon asked, looming over the back of his tech specialist as he spoke.

"The program is loading faster than we expected, it should be completed in about twenty minutes." The man indicated to the progress on the screen before them, "Genotech's tried to shut it down twice now, but we've managed to outmaneuver them both times."

"Excellent job," Devon patted the man roughly on the shoulder, this was the perfect way to get rid of Vince Anders and his horrible corporation. Devon had devoted his life to getting justice for his sister, who had been exposed to some of BioFirm's genetically modified pesticides and still suffered the damages caused by them. His parents had been fools, uneager to take on the corporate giant, they had accepted a buyout when Genotech had offered it. As if his sister's suffering was worth any amount of money. Devon's hand was clamped so hard on the back of the leather chair that he saw grooves in the material when he released it.

"Sir, are we sure about this?" The man before him asked uncertainly. "This gas will affect the whole city, that's thousands of people."

"Are you questioning the mission Kilbourne?" Devon glared at the man menacingly, he had hand-picked this team for this mission specifically. Every one of them had lost someone at the hands of BioFirm, or Genotech to some extent. He hadn't expected any of his chosen to want to default on the mission.

"It's not just the city sir, Riley is in that building." Kilbourne's voice became soft at the mention of the young girl. "You know she is, we saw her on the cameras when we got into the feed."

They had seen Riley when the black soldier had dived through the vent after her. Kilbourne had been manning the cameras and keeping an eye on the Response Team since they had gotten set up. Devon knew that Kilbourne had a soft spot for the kid, and he had to admit that he did too.

Riley was young and impressionable, a few caring words here and a sob story there and she had fully taken advantage of her aunt's status with Genotech to help them spy on Lindquist and Anders. Her being caught in this spill was an unforeseen accident. Devon hadn't known that TerraFirma, Genotech's market rival, had tried to obtain Caspian Black's formula while she was there.

He had been told by his contact at TerraFirma that the spill had been an accident, caused by carelessness of the agent they had secured to retrieve the sample. It was fortunate for them though, because they had thought they were capturing Black's original formula for the Black

Virus, but once they saw the results of the spill, they realized they had something very different.

Idiots, Devon thought to himself as he turned his mind back to Riley and Kilbourne's unwillingness to hurt her. He didn't want the kid getting hurt either, but this disaster was the only way they were going to get back at Genotech.

"Listen, Eddie," he began, pacing back and forth slowly as he spoke, "Riley knew she was going into a dangerous situation. She just didn't know how bad it would end up."

The other man nodded at him, none of them knew how bad things had gotten before they were contacted by TerraFirma and called in to hide their involvement with the spill. They had simply thought the kid was laying low before sending any information their way.

"But look at what she's done since the spill." Devon was proud of the survival instinct she possessed; given a little time, he'd probably invite her to join their inner circle. If she proved herself here at least. "She's survived all week with those creepy things after her, she's kept her head even around Lindquist's team and got herself a gas mask. She hasn't had a significant freak out yet, and now she's on the rooftop, away from all the action in the city."

Kilbourne was nodding along to every point he made; the kid really was resourceful. Devon continued.

"So, since she's safe up there, and we're already mid-mission, can we get on with this?" Kilbourne snapped him a salute, a gesture Devon was sure he had asked the man to stop using, and sat back down in his seat.

"Venting should begin in about twelve minutes, sir."

"Let's see how Anders gets out of this one." A cruel smile made its way across his face as he watched the loading bar fill up. Something in that smile sent a chill down Kilbourne's spine.

§

"Sir, someone's locked us out of the system," Carla reported back to Darcy. The Head of Security was currently barking orders at terrified looking junior analysts as they scuttled back and forth between programmers.

"Tell me something I don't know Carla," he said harshly, grabbing a file as it was handed off to him, signing it and casting it roughly back into different hands. They had lost outgoing contact with their Emergency Response Team almost as soon as they had entered the facility. There had been some interference in their communication.

The line had been hijacked and they had listened uneasily as someone had opened the Bunker doors, while Divya ordered them not to. They hadn't known what was in there until they had accessed the security cameras through Divya's backdoor.

"They've almost activated the system vent, Darcy." Carla wasn't usually this informal with him, but in this situation, he couldn't blame her. They had never expected the release of an experimental agent to be the problem when they had lost contact with the New Candor Facility, and now they had to deal with someone hindering their attempts to fix this mess. "If Lt. Kaur's message is correct, the city will be exposed to the virus in ten minutes."

The fuss around Darcy calmed as she relayed the new information. The implications of her statement settled in.

"Has anyone been able to reach the ERT to update them on the situation?" Darcy asked quietly. Carla could hear the barely restrained irritation at the situation in his voice.

"The storm is still peaking Darcy," Carla took the folder an analyst handed to her and rifled through it; it contained weather reports from New Candor. "It won't stop until well after midnight, besides, whoever is doing this isn't letting us talk to them. Darcy, what if they don't make it…" She had seen some of the security footage that Divya had patched through when she had sent her message. Carla had never seen people acting the way those things had. She could hardly bring herself to call them people when she had seen them rushing at the ERT and almost dragging Dante out of the elevator.

"They'll make it," came a voice filled with certainty from the crowded doorway. Ibrahim had returned from his solo mission and had finally gotten to the command center they had set up. "Kara and Divya won't let anything happen to the team. We just need to make sure they have a way out when they need it."

Carla looked to Darcy, who nodded in agreement, and she turned to bark out some orders of her own.

"Ibrahim, are the other members back as well?" The burly man nodded, they had called in all available ERT members when they had lost the ability to contact Kara's team. "Good, get your team prepped, we'll be heading into New Candor as soon as we're cleared to get a bird in the air."

"Carla, you can't be serious," Darcy interrupted their exchange, grabbing her gently by the arm, "I know your girls are out there but we need you here."

Carla looked to Ibrahim; he seemed afraid to speak his mind so she gestured to him to talk.

"Carla, Darcy is right, John will be our medic. You're more of a help here in command," the man said regrettably, looking as if he didn't want to stick around for her response. Carla knew they were right, but she hated the idea of this operation continuing without her. She wanted Divya and Anna back at the base, safe and sound.

"Fine. You'll be heading into the city without me then, be ready to fly in fifteen minutes." She grabbed Ibrahim by the jacket before he left. "You bring my girls home safe, you hear me?" He nodded briskly and took off down the corridor to round up the rest of his team. An analyst approached her cautiously with a message that she read quickly, eyes narrowing with every word. Carla raised her eyes and levelled her gaze at Darcy as she spoke her next words.

"We've got some information on who they are."

Chapter 12

June 10th, 2027 – NCF Ventilation System, 19:30

"We're cutting it close kids," Chris called down to the rest of the group as they made their way up yet another ladder. He was getting tired of the tight spaces and infinite ladders at this point. Not to mention the near constant silence they were trying to maintain. After passing something that screeched and slammed itself against the ventilation shaft a few floors down, they had tried to keep as quiet as possible. Chris had no idea what had tried to get in, but he knew it had scared the girl, Riley, since she had been the one closest to the grate at the time. He was impressed with the kid though, she hadn't freaked out or tried to run off, she had just taken a moment to calm down and continued like it was just a regular day at work.

"No need to remind us every floor Chris," Dean muttered, herding Riley before him onto the ladder; he was bringing up the rear of their little train.

"I'm just making sure we stay on schedule kiddo." Chris knew he didn't mind the nicknames; Dean didn't really have a complex about his age or anything, and to be honest, he wasn't that much younger than Chris himself. Chris just treated him like a kid because he was the newest member of their unit, second only to Anna, who had joined them well over a year ago. Anna had gone through her fair share of razzing before Dean had come along to take her place. Chris smiled as he remembered some of the pranks he had helped Divya pull on her. An image of Anna with green hair flitted through his mind, causing his grin to widen.

Maybe when they got home he'd help Div plan a victory prank, just for old time's sake. Anna would look pretty good orange.

"Move it old man," Dean called up from below him. Chris caught sight of the giant twenty painted on the side of the vent. He hauled himself off the ladder and turned to help the others. Once they were all gathered, they checked out the forked vents before them.

"Divya's map says that there's an exit to the roof about 50 feet that way," Chris pointed down the left fork, "we've got about 15 minutes to make it out of here. Everyone got their masks in place?" He eyed their small group as everyone double-checked their straps. Once they were secure, Chris lead the way down the ventilation shaft.

§

Kara was keeping an eye on Nick as Divya tried to get through to Genotech; the other woman had been at it for over a minute already and Kara wasn't sure she was having any luck.

"Come in, come in Command," Divya tried once more, adjusting a few knobs on the portable ComBox before continuing, "Do you read me? This is Emergency Response Team Alpha, Lieutenant Kaur speaking."

There was a small burst of static that had them holding their breaths, but the ComBox cut out once more.

"Div, maybe just use the regular frequency and send out our message? Maybe we can't hear them but they can hear us?" Kara suggested, looking down at the city below. So many people, just going about their average lives. They needed to get that message out before anything happened. Divya nodded and adjusted the ComBox once more.

"Command, this is ERT Lieutenant Kaur. There is a biological substance caught in stasis in the ventilation shafts, do not vent the system. I repeat, do not vent the system." Divya waited for a moment before beginning her message once again.

"This isn't working," Nick muttered, standing up roughly and stalking towards Divya. "You're not going to be able to save those people! We might as well try to survive this ourselves!" Divya didn't stop as he approached her. Kara didn't think he would attack the younger woman, but she wasn't willing to risk it.

"You need to sit down," she said, grasping him by the elbow as he went past her. "We're perfectly safe up here, and we need to get this message out if there's any hope of saving this city."

"But that's what I'm saying!" Nick shouted into her face, "there *is* no hope of saving this city!" Kara ground her teeth; he had been so quiet for the past few minutes that she had almost forgotten how cowardly he really was.

"Sit down Wilson, and if you're not going to be helpful, you can shut up too." Kara shoved him not too gently in the direction of the doors. Nick stumbled, caught himself, and turned around with a huff. He stormed off to a point on the roof far enough away, but still in sight of the two ladies.

Too afraid to be far from us, not that I blame him, Kara hadn't seen fit to give the man a weapon, not after she'd seen him practically sacrifice Anna to survive. She wouldn't put it past him to shoot wildly and injure someone in the process.

Clang! She heard something metallic hitting the rough gravel of the rooftop. In seconds, Nick was back at her side, Divya as well with her weapon drawn.

"Boy, does it ever feel good to be out of that cramped space!" She heard a familiar voice whisper empathically.

"Chris!" It had to be Chris and Dante. Kara rounded the raised building entrance and saw an unfamiliar, young face crawling out of the vent behind Chris.

That's right, Divya said they had found a survivor. Kara stopped a few feet away from them and waited until Chris turned to her before launching herself into his arms. The night's events hadn't fully caught up to her, and she was sure she'd need more than a sip of whiskey after this, but for now, she could content herself with the fact that her team was coming back together.

As they embraced, she watched Dante crawl out of the vent, assisted by the lanky guy. Then a small girl who ran to Divya as soon as she was out. Finally, Dean dragged himself out. Divya patted the girl on the shoulders as she looked at Dean. Kara saw him looking around and caught his eyes. She knew what he was asking and shook her head slightly to indicate that no, Anna wasn't there.

Dean's mouth twitched in the slightest frown and he walked over to Divya. The small girl had unlatched herself and had taken off her mask to clean her tears away. Kara watched as Dean reached Divya and took her into his arms. The petite woman didn't lose her hard exterior as he held her, but Kara could tell that she gladly accepted the comfort.

"Kara, where's Anna?" Chris whispered, his arm still draped across her shoulder.

"She didn't make it," was all Kara could say. There wasn't any time to get choked up now. She felt Chris stiffen beside her and watched Dante's face fall. The other two civilians seemed to sense that something was wrong, and Kara saw them slip away, allowing the team some privacy. Kara explained to the three men what had happened. At the end, Dean's grip on Divya had only tightened and Dante had wandered off to the two young survivors. Chris approached her and put a hand on her shoulder.

"It's not your fault, you know that right?" Yea, she knew, but that would never stop her from blaming herself.

"Does it make a difference whose fault it is? She's still gone." Kara allowed him to comfort her, she rested her head on his shoulder and took a few deep breaths. She heard Divya at the ComBox repeating her missive to Genotech and straightened up.

"We need to get out of here." Chris nodded at her statement. Kara was making her way to Divya's side when the announcement began.

"This is a message from Genotech. Please do not be alarmed. You are not at risk. Venting procedures have been activated. Have a pleasant day." Kara stopped and grabbed her mask, securing it in place; she shouted to the other to do the same.

"This is a message from Genotech. Please do not be alarmed. You are not at risk. Venting procedures have been activated. Have a pleasant day."

Kara joined Divya and Dean at the edge of the rooftop as they peered frantically out at the city. She looked back and watched Dante toss a mask to Nick, who dragged it roughly over his head, scraping his face badly in the process.

Thank god this stuff needs to be inhaled she thought as she watched the furrows fill with blood and drip onto Nick's dirty white shirt.

Below them, the city continued as normal. As they watched, the large, rectangular vents along the base of the compound opened. Kara looked on, horrified, as the opalescent gas shot out of the vents and settled onto the city below.

Aftermath

The streets of New Candor City are lively at night; the lights are bright and the roads are busy. Tonight, there is a haze of mist haloing the streetlights and a shock can be felt in the air. Street vendors line the corners peddling their sweets and wares to citizens who are out on the town, enjoying their night.

The gas is unnoticed at first.

Some citizens believe it to be a fast-moving fog bank, which isn't uncommon in this city, as the humid life below usually interacts with the cooler mountain air and causes a lot of strange weather phenomenon. Like this electrical storm for instance, it is the third for the month they have had. It is an inconvenience, since storms like this tend to knock out cellphone and radio communication in the city, but most towns have their issues.

Citizens of New Candor get to enjoy a thriving economy provided by the biotechnology firm Genotech, and if they had to live with the occasional blaring siren or warning due to an alarm test, they can deal with it. The pleasant lady on the announcement tells them to stay calm, that this is a test, and they listen.

Why wouldn't they?

When the first citizen drops, gagging on something invisible and clawing at the skin of his throat, people are uneasy. No one knows if they should approach him, or if they can help him. There are officers nearby, as they usually are when these electrical storms hit. Their radios are at a low frequency and they can communicate during emergencies.

As an officer reaches for his radio, he starts feeling the effects of the gas. His breath catches in his throat and it constricts. He can feel his eyes bulging in their sockets as his body reacts to the almost instant, loss of oxygen. He scrapes at his constricted throat and reaches out to his partner, who is now convulsing in the seat beside him. If he could only reach the speaker, they may get help in time. His grasping hands knock the speaker from its cradle and it falls to the floor. He can hear their dispatcher calling over the radio faintly.

"Unit 702, what's your handle? Unit 702, come in, Barry are you there?" He wonders why they sound so faint, then he realizes that it's because he is losing consciousness. Everything is swimming and the clawed hands he sees before him are covered in blood.

That's mine… he thinks, looking over to his partner once more. There's a line of frothy, red drool dripping from the corner of his mouth. His eyes are rolled back so far that all Barry can see are bloodshot whites. He loses consciousness looking out the windshield at the citizens around him; someone has crashed their vehicle and there are electrical wires dangling over the street. His last sight is the image of a woman, crawling in the streets and gasping for air. The electrical wire comes down on her and she convulses violently, her hair going up in a lick of flame so bright it hurts his eyes, her face frozen in a silent scream she can't voice. He finds it funny as he closes his eyes.

I thought that only happens in movies...

Then it's quiet. There is the sound of car alarms blaring and the crackling of flames that are eating the bodies of vehicles and whatever is trapped within them. The only sound is a pleasant, automated voice, echoing through the air.

"We at Genotech thank you for your co-operation. Venting procedures are now complete. Have a lovely day."

§

"Ok team, we've got a lot of civilians down there who are unaware of what is going on. They will be panicked; they will be scared." Ibrahim had briefed the team as quickly as he could on what they would be encountering when they got down to ground level. Carla had come in to explain the extent of the effects of the gas, and he could see the reactions of each individual team member etched on their harshly lit faces. His own reaction was one of mild disgust at the experiments he had learned about. "First thing's first, we meet up with Team Alpha at the New Candor Facility. Once they are secured, we move on to evacuation and extermination."

"Extermination, Sir?" John, "So we're sure there's no way to save these people?" Ibrahim shook his head. Carla had told him that in all tests performed on live subjects, there had been no incidence of the subjects reverting to their original state.

"No John, there's no other way." They were five minutes from their landing point, they would be going in hot from the rooftop of the New Candor Facility, and would be heading down to the lab, where they had last known the Alpha team to be. The chopper crested its last mountain range and Ibrahim inhaled a sharp spike of breath.

The city before them was glowing a sickly orange. Not to say that the entire city was on fire, but he could spot various major blazes that were struggling to be put out. They flew over a firetruck that spewed water onto a burning building and Ibrahim watched as police officers formed a loose ring around the overworked firemen and took out monsters leaping towards them. The downwash from the chopper's rotors seemed to make the blaze worse, as it suddenly flared up, devouring the half of the building it hadn't yet consumed.

"Captain." John didn't need to say anything else. They were needed, and this was as good a place as any to help. He would explain it to Kara later, when they were debriefing, and she would understand his decision. He made his way to the PIC and signaled for him to take them down at the nearest patch of clear ground. The pilot banked their chopper towards a park and Ibrahim saw the danger. He reacted faster than he thought he could. The gas station they flew over hadn't been one of the ones on fire, but a line of flame had made its way to the large propane tanks. He threw himself onto his seat and shoved the buckles of his belt together just in time.

"Duck and cover!" He shouted to his men, who rolled in on themselves and covered their heads with their arms as twin, blinding lights bloomed below them. Ibrahim felt the chopper jerk in the air and heard the muted screech of metal as the rotors bent. His stomach disappeared somewhere in the back of his throat as they dropped out of the air. The concussive blast made everything seem surreal, as everything came down around him in slow motion, with sounds muffled and muted by the damage to his eardrums. The crash jerked him around in the belt; he tried to keep his focus and looked up in time to see one of his men torn from his seat and launched out the broken door. Ibrahim reached weakly for the man before the chopper came to a jerky halt. The last thing he felt was a blistering heat across his face and chest.

The fuel tank, was all he could think as he felt himself thrown backwards, the blasts battering his eardrums once more.

§

Divya held on to the glove Kara had given her as they watched the gas spread across the city. Genotech's venting system extended through the city and out into the surrounding area. The system was intended to vent water vapor, which was what the gas was supposed to revert to once it was collected. She had realized something was wrong with the system when they were in the lab. Some of the holding tanks were offline due to maintenance and the captured gas had been trapped in the humid ventilation shafts. She couldn't see the people in the streets below, but the gas was settling in.

"Divya!" Kara's voice was sharp; it probably wasn't the first time she had called Divya's name.

"Yes Captain." She turned away from the devastation. She could remain professional, she was hurting over the loss of Anna and irritated over her own failure to stop Genotech, but professionalism was her fallback and she could handle this. "Sorry, what did you ask?"

"I need you to fill us in on the effects of this outbreak; what should we expect once we're down there?" Kara was giving her something to hold on to. If she was helping the others, she wouldn't have to deal with the loss. Not until they were safe at home at least.

"The gas will settle and dissipate slowly over the next four hours. This storm is keeping the air heavy; we can't even rely on a strong wind to help us. Any civilians not already exposed will be vulnerable to exposure if they're not protected," she gestured to her gas mask. "Unfortunately, we don't have nearly enough of these for all those people down there. Our best bet is to get an emergency announcement out to the citizens as soon as possible. Warn them to cover all openings, keep them safe from further exposure. Once we get to a radio tower we can do that, and contact Genotech to call in the other teams too."

"So, we need to get to The Bus then?" Chris asked. "Not going to be so easy with all those things in the building."

"Don't worry big guy, there are a lot more of us going down than there were coming up!" Dean slugged Chris in the arm and the bigger man feigned a look of shock at the smile on Dean's face.

"Wait, *you're* trying to cheer *me* up? Are you seeing this Cap?" Chris asked, pointing wildly at Dean. "Do you see what he's trying to do to me?" Kara smiled at Chris's antics and turned to Divya.

"We do need to get down there, don't we?" Divya nodded at Kara, her grip on Anna's glove tightening.

"We need to make a stop at the lab to re-stock too, we're running low on ammo. I think we had a few extra masks too, might come in handy?" Divya turned to look out at the city once again. She hated the idea that they might come across Anna down there, but she needed to be ready if it happened. She brought the glove to her lips for a moment, held it there and then tucked it carefully into her vest.

"So, are we leaving then?" The man, Nick, spoke up, "it's about time you people decide to do something! How are you going to keep us safe if you can't even keep each other safe though?" He gestured to himself and the other two civilians. Divya could see Kara take a step towards him out of the corner of her eye. The dig about Anna hurt, but she would deal with that later.

"My good man, you'll be with me," Chris said, wrapping an arm around Nick and pulling him aside gently. "I'm the biggest guy here, those things will have trouble getting to you with me in the way." This seemed to comfort the man and he allowed himself to be taken away from Kara's reach.

"Alright, Riley, you're with Dean and Divya," Kara barked out. "Evan, you're with Dante and myself."

"What about me?" Nick shouted from a few feet away, "why do I only get one person?!"

"Buddy, you don't need anyone else, I'm the best on the team!" Chris's grin was stretched too far on his face, Divya could tell he didn't like the guy, but he didn't want Kara to do anything she'd regret either.

"Fine, if it's just going to be the two of us, I want a weapon." Divya ground her teeth, she could sympathize with Kara now. This guy was annoying.

And Anna sacrificed herself for him? The thought cooled her emotions. Anna had put her duty before her emotions, and they would all follow that example.

"He can have this," Riley stepped up and held out her pistol by the muzzle. Nick made a grab for the weapon and almost managed to pull the trigger in his haste.

"Hey! Watch it!" Dean ordered as he yanked Riley out of the sight of the gun.

"I know what I'm doing," Nick rolled his eyes as he made a shooing motion with the weapon. Divya was nervous just watching his casual handling of a loaded gun. "Let's get out of here, the faster we're done, the faster I can get out of this nightmare." The team looked to Kara one by one. Their Captain was pale, and looking like she was about to deck the man. Divya caught her eye and nodded, she understood what Kara was dealing with. This man would make trouble for them if they took the weapon away, and trouble was something they didn't need right now. She wished Riley hadn't stepped up so quickly with a weapon.

"Alright," Kara started, "Let's get to the lab, then we head down to the garage." The team assembled and they made their way into the dark building once again.

A pleasant voice wafted through the air as the door shut behind them.

"We at Genotech thank you for your co-operation. Venting procedures are now complete. Have a lovely day."

BLACK VIRUS OUTBREAK

Epilogue:
Black Virus: Survival

She scuttled along the narrow shaft, scraping her knees occasionally on the cold metal. She had fallen at some point, baring her knees to the elements. She had had weapons at some point as well, but they were long gone. The only means of protection left was a small pocket knife she kept hidden away, just in case.

Well, this looks exactly like a 'just in case' type of situation, she thought as she passed another dark turn off. She peered into the murky darkness, hoping to catch a glimpse of light at the end, indicating the roof exit.

Nothing to be seen.

She continued down the tight space, praying for a point where the tunnel would widen up. As she crawled along, she kept an eye on the grates beside her. This section of the ventilation shafts was at ground level in the corridor, and she didn't want to attract the attention of anything while she was weaponless. She heard a sound and froze. There was a soft chuffing noise coming from the grate ahead. She crept forward slowly, being careful not to make a sound, not wanting to draw any attention to the grate. The noise continued. It almost sounded like someone crying. She reached the grate and risked peeking outside.

There was a figure standing in the darkened hallway. She could see the spotty lab coat and assumed this was one of the affected scientists, a thrall. As she watched, the figured turned around, ever so slowly. It was as if it was trying to walk through molasses. She didn't doubt that this thing would attack her if she were to try to run past it. She didn't need to get out of the shaft here though, she still needed to find the roof exit and meet the group upstairs. She pulled back from the grate as another figure appeared at the end of the hallway.

This was a different thrall altogether. She had seen one of these before. She cringed as the thing began tearing at its ears, letting out an eerie moan as they began to bleed. The thrall she had been observing before sprang to life as soon as the other creature appeared.

Movement.

That's what triggered these things. Movement faster than their own basic speed prompted an inhuman change in their passive behaviour. At one moment, they would be wading through the air, as though it was filled with molasses. The next moment, they would be on top of anyone who caught their attention. Something to do with a deteriorated frontal cortex, she would assume. She watched in silent horror as the thrall attacked the newcomer, tearing at him with its clawed hands, ripping new gouges into his already bloody skin. The newcomer went crazy, he began screeching in an animalistic fashion, sounding insanely close to an agitated primate and ripped into the thrall.

It was over in seconds. She watched at the thrall dropped to the floor, one hand still clawed, ripping down the front of the other's suit. She held her breath, waiting for the other to leave. She didn't know what triggered these ones yet. She had encountered her first mutant a few hours ago. Her heart hammered in her chest as she waited. She watched the thing begin to twitch and scratch at it's ears once more. It took a step towards the grate and she backed up, bumping into the far wall, cloth on metal. The mutant thrall dove towards the grate, starting up that gibbering screech once more. She surged forward, not wanting to get caught on the wrong side of the grate when it broke in. She crawled along as fast as she could, hearing the thing screeching and cringing at the distinct sound of fingernails on metal.

Ladder, ladder, ladder, come on, tell me there's a way out of here, she thought frantically as she crawled, peeking down each turn for a sign of light.

The grate came off with a metallic screech, she could hear the thing practically slobbering as it came up the shaft in her direction. She couldn't think of how it knew where she was, she hadn't left much of a trail, unless it was tracking her by scent. She didn't know enough about these creatures.

She looked down another turn and almost continued before she realized what she had seen. Up ahead, there was a faint glow. She ground her teeth and began scuttling forward, listening out for the progress of the thrall behind her. If she could make it out before it caught up, she wouldn't be caught in a knife fight with a creature that didn't need a knife.

She made her way further down the shaft and realized that there was more space now. She continued crawling for a few more feet, before it opened enough for her to stand up and run along at a crouch. In this position, it was much easier to move quickly. She listened behind her for sounds of the thrall and panicked when she realized how much closer the thing had gotten. The small space didn't seem to bother its movements as much as it did hers. It probably helped that the thing didn't care if it left chunks of itself behind.

The walls widened until she stood in, what looked like, an electrical room. She could see pipes running along the walls from the shaft, leading further ahead before taking a turn upwards. Looking up, she could see a hatch and a short ladder on the far wall of the room. She hid her grin and ran over to the ladder. If she could get out before the thrall made it here she'd be fine. At the top of the ladder she saw the latch. She grabbed her knife, pressed the button to expose the blade and began prying at the flimsy latch.

The sounds were closer; she could practically hear each step he took down the narrow shaft. Once she had gotten the knife wedged into the lock, she began wriggling it back and forth, loosening the already weak screws.

She was focussed on her task and didn't realize how quiet it had gotten. She looked down from the ladder and the mutated thrall stood in the shaft entrance.

She stopped.

She could feel her heart rate increasing. As it did, she realized that the thrall had started scratching at its ears once more. She managed to slip the knife from the latch and readied herself for the inevitable lunge.

Within seconds the thrall had crossed the room. She barely had time to react before it had grabbed her ankle and hauled her off the ladder. She fell to the floor with a thud and a metallic clang, feeling a pain sear immediately through her right shoulder. She gasped loudly at the pain and the thrall began screeching once more. She pushed herself up and rolled away as the thrall brought both fists down where she had been, as if it intended to pummel her to death. Its behaviour reminded her of the apes in the mammal trials. She looked around for the knife that had slipped out of her hand when she landed and saw it behind him.

Of course, she didn't have time to think anything else before he was on her again, this time clawing furiously at her chest, as if trying to rip her heart clean out. She fought the numbness of her shoulder and brought her arms up between them. With all the force she could muster she thrust an open palm directly at his nose, angling her hit as best she could in the close quarters. It was enough for him to stagger back slightly, allowing her enough room to scoot backwards. Her shirt had protected her from any real damage, but as she looked down she could make out faint bits of flesh and, what looked like fingernails caught in the material. She held back the urge to gag. The knife was still out of reach she could see, he had made his way between her and her weapon once again. Thinking quickly, she pushed herself off the ground and dashed towards the walls. The pipes here were thin, and looked as if the could be pried off easily. She wasted no time.

The mutant thrall came at her again, screeching his gibberish and clawing at his ears as she pried a two-foot long length of pipe from the wall. She felt her nail tear but paid no attention as she whirled around to meet him. It was over quickly. She held the pipe out, angled upwards, as it rushed her. She felt a slight resistance, and then heard a wet pop as it made its way into the thrall's skull. She let go of the pipe immediately, not wanting to feel the life drain on the end of the makeshift spear any longer.

She knew she'd never forget what it felt like.

She walked over to the knife and checked the blade. She could hear whimpers and mewling behind her.

"I'm sorry..." Was all she could think to say as she made her way up the ladder, popped the latch, and made her way onto the rooftop. She shut the door behind her and looked around. She saw a large rock by one of the doors to the roof and brought it over to hold the hatch shut.

Finally, she sat down and took in her surroundings. She had heard the announcement a while ago and had been relieved to have her gas mask on during the vent. She walked to the edge of the roof and looked out into the city.

There were columns of smoke rising in different areas of the city. If Divya had been right, the gas would take almost four hours to dissipate, meaning that anyone still outside without a mask could still be affected. As she looked out, she saw movement on the asphalt below. The Humvees moved in a straight line, heading out of the building. She had a decent idea of who was in them. She looked around, hoping to see the portable ComBox that Kara had been carrying. Nothing.

Her teammates were survivalists. She was sure that they hadn't been able to contact Genotech. If they had, Carla would have told them to stay put, and sent a chopper to pick them up. They would have needed a sure way to contact Genotech, if the ComBox failed, and Anna knew just where Divya would lead them.

She needed to get downstairs. There were weapons in Lab 4, if they left any, and she could possibly find some keys in the security offices if she was careful enough. Anna made her way to the fire escape.